CAST OF CHARACTERS

Jarod Bodine: an oh-so-respectable single-dad rancher...except for one momentary lapse—a torrid night with Susan Mitchell.

Susan Mitchell: a teacher with a secret...and she's got more than tutoring in mind when she shows up unexpectedly at the Bodine Ranch.

Danny Bodine: a rambunctious eight-year-old... bummed to be spending his summer in a leg cast, but his pretty new tutor is more fun than the amusement park!

Claude: the Bodine family barn cat and mouser extraordinaire.

Dear Reader,

Though each Special Edition novel is sprinkled with magic, you should know that the authors of your favorite romances are *not* magicians—they're women just like you.

"Romance is a refuge for me. It lifts my spirits." Sound familiar? That's Christine Rimmer's answer to why she reads— and writes—romance. Christine is the author of this month's *The Tycoon's Instant Daughter,* which launches our newest in-line continuity the STOCKWELLS OF TEXAS. Like you, she started out as a reader while she had a multifaceted career— actress, janitor, waitress, phone sales representative. "But I really wanted one job where I wouldn't have to work any other jobs," Christine recalls. Now, thirteen years and thirty-seven books later, Ms. Rimmer is an established voice in Special Edition.

Some other wonderful voices appear this month. Susan Mallery delivers *Unexpectedly Expecting!,* the latest in her LONE STAR CANYON series. Penny Richards's juicy series RUMOR HAS IT... continues with *Judging Justine.* It's love Italian-style with Tracy Sinclair's *Pretend Engagement,* an alluring romance set in Venice. The cat is out of the bag, so to speak, in Diana Whitney's *The Not-So-Secret Baby.* And young Trent Brody is hoping to see his *Beloved Bachelor Dad* happily married in Crystal Green's debut novel.

We aim to give you six novels every month that lift *your* spirits. Tell me what you like about Special Edition. What would you like to see more of in the line? Write to: Silhouette Books, 300 East 42nd St., 6th Floor, New York, NY 10017. I encourage you to be part of making your favorite line even better!

Best,

Karen Taylor Richman
Senior Editor

Please

The Not-So-Secret Baby

DIANA WHITNEY

SPECIAL EDITION™

Published by Silhouette Books

America's Publisher of Contemporary Romance

To Claude the cat, my grandkitty, and to my son Jeff, who responds to Claude's every meow with an immediate "Yes, master?" Hugs to you both!

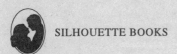 SILHOUETTE BOOKS

ISBN 0-373-24373-1

THE NOT-SO-SECRET BABY

Copyright © 2001 by Diana Hinz

This edition published by arrangement with Harlequin Books S.A.

Visit Silhouette at www.eHarlequin.com

Printed in U.S.A.

DIANA WHITNEY

A three-time Romance Writers of America RITA Award finalist, *Romantic Times Magazine* Reviewers' Choice nominee and finalist for Colorado Romance Writers' Award of Excellence, Diana has published more than two dozen romance and suspense novels since her first Silhouette title in 1989. A popular speaker, Diana has conducted writing workshops and has published several articles on the craft of fiction writing for various trade magazines and newsletters. She is a member of Authors Guild, Novelists, Inc., Published Authors Network and Romance Writers of America. She and her husband live in rural Northern California with a beloved menagerie of furred creatures, domestic and wild. She loves to hear from readers. You can write to her c/o Silhouette Books, 300 East 42nd Street, 6th Floor, New York, NY 10017.

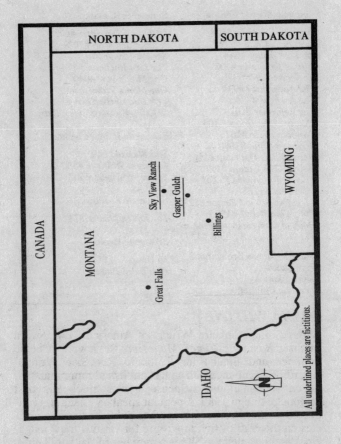

All underlined places are fictitious.

Chapter One

The scream echoed through the north pasture, startling the lame gelding whose hoof was being inspected. Another piercing shriek echoed across the Montana plains, followed by a keening wail of sheer terror. But the screams were not the cries of a dying animal; they were human.

Jarod Bodine dropped the gelding's foreleg and ran toward the ranch house as if his boots were on fire. The shrieks grew louder, more frantic. He instinctively grabbed a snake-spade propped against the warped wallboards of the old barn his great-granddaddy had built, then leaped the paddock fence and skidded to a stunned stop some fifty feet from the house.

Jarod wasn't shocked to see a woman on his front porch. Applicants for the job of tutoring his injured son had been popping up all week. This woman, however, was howling at the top of her lungs, flailing wildly and stamping her feet as if performing a primitive war dance.

An appreciative hoot from the porch caught Jarod's attention. "Jump higher!" Seated in his hated wheelchair with his left leg immobilized in the plaster cast he'd be stuck with for the next few weeks, eight-year-old Danny cheered her on. "Try spinning around, and stamp your feet real hard!"

On cue, the female whirled and stamped as if auditioning for a Celtic dance troupe. From Jarod's vantage point, he saw only a vague blond blur of movement, but was unable to view what provoked the peculiar mayhem or catch more than a glimpse of a face concealed behind a glossy swish of hair.

"Help me!" the woman shrieked to no one in particular. "Get it out, get it o-o-out!" She stamped, spun, screamed then slapped at the front of her form-fitting skirt before beginning the peculiar ritual all over again. Only when she'd gyrated her way down the wooden steps did Jarod notice the stalking creature following close on her heels, then circling her ankles with predatory intent.

It was Claude, the cat.

Danny wheeled to the edge of the porch ramp, clearly delighted by the performance. "Man, that's like, so totally cool! I never saw anybody who could do stuff like that before."

The woman responded with a high-pitched howl, hopped from one high-heeled foot to the other, then violently shook her hips in a manner that reminded Jarod of a hula-hoop contest he'd once witnessed at the state fair.

Suddenly the woman let out a horrified whoop, spun around until her back was to him, then went absolutely rigid. Simultaneously a small, furred creature emerged from the hem of her skirt.

Claude leaped forward.

The creature scampered down the woman's leg, bounced from the toe of her feminine, but ranch-inappropriate mid-heel pump, and dashed toward a nearby bundle of buckbrush with the exuberant feline right on its tail.

Moaning in relief, the woman drooped like a rag doll. Still facing away from Jarod, she curled forward, bracing herself with her hands on her thighs. The movement stretched the fabric of her nicely tailored skirt across a posterior that was enticing enough to catch a lonely widower's attention. A delicate shudder vibrated shapely shoulders clad in a silky, ivory-colored blouse.

"Well," she murmured in an embarrassed voice that barely reached Jarod's ears. "That was…interesting."

Danny managed to speak between howls of laughter. "That was so awesome. You were really moving."

The woman straightened, tossed her head so the hair that had been cascading forward swished back into a shiny tumble extending down to her shoulder blades. She raised her arm and appeared to be brushing stray strands from her face. "Quite an aerobic workout, that. Nothing like an indiscreet rodent to reveal hidden talents."

A quiver of good humor lightened her tone. Jarod could tell she was smiling. A vague sense of déjà vu slipped through his mind, only to dissipate as he strained to hear her next words.

"Ah, my hero," she murmured as a disappointed

Claude meandered back, sans mouse, to rub against her ankles. She bent to pet the animal, a charcoal tabby cat built like a squat, furred tank. "Not that I didn't appreciate the gift and the pride you displayed while presenting it. I'm just not that fond of rodents, you see."

Claude gazed up adoringly.

"Claude's a really good barn cat," Danny told her. "He even kills rattlesnakes sometimes. Dad's worried he's gonna get bit, but Claude's a lot smarter than any stupid snake."

A note of caution crept into her voice. "Speaking of your father, do you know when he might be back? I realize I'm late, but when I was told this place was forty miles from town, I had no idea that thirty of those miles were on unpaved, unmarked dirt roads. I halfway expected to run into a wagon train or a war party."

Rubber wheelchair tires rumbled on the newly constructed ramp at the side of the porch. "Yeah, we're really out in the sticks." Danny rolled to the edge of the ramp, but no farther. The child hadn't ventured farther than the front porch since the accident. "There's nothing to do out here, nobody to play with. I hate it."

Jarod flinched at the sting in the child's tone. A cold fist of fear clamped around his heart. He was losing him, Jarod realized, losing his son. The thought terrified him.

"This land has a quiet beauty," the woman was saying. "I can see why you'd be lonely sometimes, especially since the accident, but this place is incredibly special." As she spoke, she placed her hands on her hips, tossed her hair, and appeared to be gazing out over the vista of wild plateaus and rugged plains that extended as far as the eye could see. "Such a magnificent view."

The ramp planks creaked as Danny pivoted his wheelchair. "Dad says that Bodines have owned Sky View Ranch for a hundred years, and the land is in our blood." He said with a snort, "It's not in my blood. Nothing but dust and rocks and—" he shuddered audibly "—and big, ugly horses. My mom hated it, too, only she was too nice to say anything, so Dad didn't know."

The fist of emotion clamped around Jarod's heart tightened to the point of physical pain. He'd known how his wife had felt about the ranch. God help him, he'd always known, but had feigned ignorance so he wouldn't have to choose between the woman he adored and the land that was as much a part of him as his skin.

It had been a coward's way out, he supposed. Jarod had always meant to talk to Gail about their life here, find out exactly what she'd needed to be happy. But he'd put it off, fearing her answer and convincing himself that it had never been the right time for such a deep discussion.

Then time had run out.

An excited voice brought Jarod back from the past. "There he is! Hey, Dad! You shoulda seen what Claude did! He chased a mouse right up Miss Mitchell's skirt, and…"

The rest of his son's delighted description just sailed right over Jarod's head as the woman in question turned toward him. His breath caught in his throat, his chest tightened into a searing knot and he felt boneless enough that a newborn foal could have knocked him over with a snort.

The woman's gaze locked with his. A flicker of emotion pinched her gentle features, but only for a moment. She tilted her head slightly, as if sizing him up.

When she finally spoke, her voice was soft, pleasant. Cautious. "Good afternoon, Mr. Bodine."

Jarod didn't recall asking his feet to move, although he was suddenly standing barely five feet away from her. He never took his eyes off her face. "Danny, would you excuse us, please?"

"How come? You always let me talk to the tutors."

"Do as I ask, son."

"But—"

"Now." The final word brooked no argument. Jarod heard his son's annoyed mutter, the scuff of rubber wheels on the hollow-planked porch, followed by the squeak of hinges and the slam of a door.

Silence descended like a dusty shroud.

For what seemed a small eternity, neither of them spoke. They simply stared at each other with wary eyes—and something else, something deeper, more profound.

Jarod finally found his voice. "So, it's Miss Mitchell, is it?"

Her smile was a little sad. "Yes, Mitchell. Susan Mitchell. I'd hoped you might remember."

He nodded. "I'm sorry. I didn't recognize you—" He bit off the words, but not soon enough.

Visibly pale, she lowered her voice, and finished the sentence for him. "With my clothes on?"

"Something like that." He set his jaw, clenched his fists at his side.

Damn. It was going to be one of those days.

* * *

He wasn't the man she remembered.

That man had been vulnerable and giving, gentle and kind. His eyes had glowed with soft interest, secret sadness, a warmth that was missing from the cold, gray gaze now raking her with tangible suspicion.

"What are you doing here?" The question was flung like a sharpened dart, swift and on target.

A flutter along her left eyelid signaled the extent of her tension. She hoped he wouldn't notice. "The school district sent me. I'm a teacher, remember?"

A flash of recall flickered through his cool gaze, then disappeared with a blink. "We had an agreement."

Susan kept her gaze level, her expression impassive. "I understand."

He shifted, hooked his thumbs in his jeans' pockets and gazed across the sprawling Montana landscape. "If you've come here looking for an apology, you've got it."

For some reason, that hurt. "As chivalrous as it is for you to shoulder full responsibility for what happened between us, the fact is that we jointly chose a course of action that in retrospect was far from prudent. Regardless, this is neither a social call nor an invitation to sing 'Auld Lang Syne.' It's a job interview. Your son requires the services of a tutor until he can return to the classroom. My credentials in that regard are impeccable. You want the best. I am the best. Case closed."

Eyebrows too straight and bushy to be considered handsome hitched, then lowered into a furry frown. There was no glow of amusement in Jarod's wintry eyes, only an icy stare of suspicion. "Another display of that appealing modesty, I see."

Her skin heated to the point of discomfort. It took all of her willpower not to spill the irksome moisture gathering in her eyes. "I didn't come here to insult you, Mr. Bodine, or to be insulted by you."

He blinked, poked his wide-brimmed hat back with his thumb and stared at the ground. "That was ungentlemanly of me. I apologize. Again." He looked up, his eyes still cool but wary rather than angry.

For a brief moment, Susan glimpsed the vulnerability she remembered. But only for a moment. Then he narrowed his stare, clamped his jaw and avoided her gaze.

Susan didn't blame him. Job or no job, she knew perfectly well that even her presence here was a violation of the agreement they'd made three months ago in a darkened pub on the outskirts of the county.

Susan had never gone to a pub or bar unescorted before. She'd done so that night deliberately, perhaps perversely, the culmination of a miserable week when the fellow she'd been dating for two years had calmly announced he was engaged to someone else.

That stunning development had followed an excited phone call from her youngest sister, Catrina, announcing that she too was about to get married to the man of her dreams. Since Susan's eldest sister, Laura, had found her own Prince Charming recently, Susan seemed destined to be the odd-woman out of the Cinderella sisters syndrome.

Of course, Susan had always been the pragmatic one, the disdainful adolescent who'd eschewed romantic fantasy for the harsh realities of her formative years, realities that included a father who'd abandoned the family shortly after Susan had been born, followed by a stepfather who'd done the same thing five years later, leaving only sour memories and a baby sister to remember him by.

So, on a cold and lonely winter night Susan had drowned her troubles in a few beers and shared an intimate night with a sad-eyed stranger, a night so passionate the memory still raised gooseflesh.

She couldn't explain the dynamics of that experience. Perhaps it had begun with the melancholy music from the soft country band or the seductive atmosphere of the darkened pub filled with quiet strangers. Perhaps it was simply the combination of alcohol, loneliness and a kindred spirit with which to share both.

Afterwards, they'd agreed the liaison had been a pleasant diversion that should be tucked neatly into a drawer of fond memories and kept private.

Which is exactly where Susan would have left them had those sweet hours of carnal bliss not produced something more substantial than fond memories.

So Susan had come seeking more than a job, just as Jarod clearly suspected. Susan had come seeking answers, answers she sadly discovered in the hard glare of a gaze that revealed none of the gentleness she remembered, none of the vulnerability that had touched her heart just a few short months ago.

She moistened her lips, absently touched her midsection. "From your expression I'd judge that you'd rather be staked on a fire-ant hill than give me the job."

"That about sums it up."

"In that case, good day to you, Mr. Bodine."

Susan left without a backwards glance. She told her-

self that it didn't matter, that she hadn't really expected Jarod Bodine to be different from the other
emotionally detached men who had shifted into and
out of her life. Besides, children grew up without fathers all the time. Susan and her sisters had, and they
had turned out fine, just fine.

Susan didn't need Jarod Bodine. She didn't need
anybody.

So why was she crying?

"Where's she going?" Danny wheeled away from
the window as Jarod entered the house. "How come
you didn't bring Miss Mitchell inside to talk to me?
I'm supposed to talk to them all. You promised, you
promised."

Angry and frustrated, the child tried to pivot around
his father, who was deliberately blocking the front
door.

Jarod avoided his son's gaze. "She wasn't right for
the job, Danny."

"Yes, she was!" Danny pounded his fist on the arm
of his chair. "She was just right! She has smiley eyes
and a cool laugh, and she likes cats, even cats that
give her mice. She doesn't smell like mothballs, she
doesn't get all puckered around the mouth when I tell
her jokes, and she didn't glare at me like I'm some
kind of dweeb when I said I don't like homework. She
said that she never liked homework either."

The thrum of a car engine confirmed that the
woman in question was leaving. Jarod angled a glance
out the window, stepped away from the door only
when he saw dust spit from tires as the vehicle lum-
bered down the rutted driveway toward the main road.

Heaving a sigh, Jarod removed his hat, wiped his

brow with his forearm. "You'll have to trust me, son. Miss Mitchell wasn't the right teacher for you."

"You mean she wasn't the right teacher for *you*," the boy shot back. "I saw the way you looked at her."

Jarod straightened cautiously. "What do you mean?"

"You looked at her the way you looked at that guy who was selling cattle prods and horse hobbles." Danny pushed his lower lip out, a gesture designed to make the most of single-parent-guilt syndrome and effectively used by a motherless child who had spent the past four years perfecting the process. "You made her go away without even giving her a chance."

"I...talked to her."

"For two minutes." Danny pivoted his chair around, and rolled to the window. "You promised I could choose. You promised."

Jarod flopped his hat on a nearby wall hook, raked his fingers through hair gritty with dust. Another point of fatherhood he'd just managed to screw up royally.

Danny was an obstinate child, frequently contentious and always willful. If Jarod said "left," Danny automatically said "right." By dismissing the lovely Miss Mitchell out of hand, he'd played right into his son's contrary nature. He should have known better; did know better, in fact.

If he hadn't been so stunned and horrified by Susan Mitchell's unexpected reappearance in his life he would have handled the situation a hell of a lot better.

At least, he hoped that he would have.

"You're right, Danny, we'd agreed that you'd make the final decision, and I shouldn't have sent her away without discussing the matter with you. The next time, I'll—"

"There isn't gonna be a next time." The boy glanced over his shoulder with angry eyes and a clamp to his jaw that made Jarod's heart sink. "If I can't have Miss Mitchell, I don't want anybody."

"You won't be able to attend regular classes for the rest of the school year, Danny. If you don't keep up your grades, you won't be able to move into the fourth grade next fall with the rest of your classmates."

"Who cares?"

"I care."

"Well, I don't." Danny returned his gaze to the window. "Momma would have let me choose my own teacher. She'd never break a promise, either."

That was a low blow.

Jarod spun on his boot heel, went into the kitchen and yanked a beer from the fridge. He slammed the refrigerator door, propped a hip against the kitchen counter.

A few feet away, a portly woman with a pinched frown busied herself paring potatoes. Jarod glanced at her. "Go ahead and say it."

Martha West, who was married to Jarod's ranch foreman and had run two households with an iron fist for the past four years, favored him with a bland stare. "I've nothing to say on the matter. Danny's your boy, and you're raising him the best you can."

"I sense a 'but' in there."

"No 'buts.'" She laid down the paring knife, wiped her hands on her apron. "You're a fine father, and Danny's a fine boy. A tad bullheaded, he is, and a wee bit spoiled, but 'tis to be expected with one who has suffered such tragic loss so early in life."

Jarod popped the beer-can top, took a healthy swallow of the sharp brew. It slipped down his throat, delightfully bitter, pungent, just the way he liked it. "How much did you overhear?"

"All of it, I imagine. Except the conversation you had with the teacher out front." A small twinkle lit her pale gaze. "My eyesight is failing. Lipreading isn't as easy as once it was, though I saw enough, what with the two of you circling each other like hungry foxes claiming the last hen in the coop. Met her before, have you?"

He flinched. "It was that obvious?"

"Only to one of extraordinary perception and unfortunate longevity such as myself. 'Tis hell to get old, but the wisdom of it offers some advantages."

"You're not old, Martha, and neither is Samuel. I couldn't run this place without the two of you."

Her smile widened at the mention of her husband, a curmudgeonly old codger who could outride, outrope and outrun anyone on the ranch, including Jarod himself.

"Aye," Martha said with a wink, "and don't you be forgetting that."

"Not a chance."

A slam from the parlor startled Jarod.

"You said I could choose," Danny shouted from the other room. "You lied to me."

Jarod groaned, chugged another swallow of beer, wiped his mouth with the sleeve of his shirt. "I've really screwed this up. I should have insisted that that woman was the one I was going to hire. Then he'd have pitched a fit and refused to have anything to do with her. You'd think by now I'd have an inkling of how to deal with my own son's contrary nature."

"'Tisn't your way," Martha said simply. "You're

not a man to manipulate folks when an honest response will work.''

"Honesty wasn't the best course of action here.''

She leveled her gaze. "And was it honesty that you offered him?''

A slow heat crawled up his throat. Jarod didn't answer, partly because Martha didn't expect him to and partly because he couldn't. Honesty hadn't been an option, not when it required explaining to Danny that his father had succumbed to a weakness of mind and body and had spent a passionate night with a beautiful stranger. How could he explain that to a child when he didn't understand it himself?

The memory of that night still lingered, haunting his dreams, taunting his lonely heart with a desire so intense that the power of it frightened him.

"So why are you thinking this young woman, whom you have obviously met before, suddenly showed up, hmm?''

Jarod blinked, glanced across the cramped-but-tidy kitchen to the crayoned pictures tacked on the mudroom door. "She said the school district sent her.''

"But you're not believing that, are you?''

A dismal shrug conveyed that he didn't know what to believe.

"'Tis good to be wary.'' Martha picked up a potato, regarded it thoughtfully, balancing it in her palm as if testing the quality of the vegetable by the feel of it. "After all, you're a fine-looking man, a good catch as the young ladies said in my day. Worth a pretty penny, you are, what with owning half the land between here and Gasper's Gulch. A woman could do worse, and that's a fact.''

Jarod managed a thin smile. "If there was a compliment buried in there, I'll accept it with thanks."

"So it's compliments you're wanting, is it?" She laughed. "Well, you'll not be getting any from me. That battered old hat of yours wouldn't fit a swelled-up head, and one spoiled Bodine around here is quite enough, thank you."

Before Jarod could reply, the jarring sound of a wheel hub scraping a corridor wall announced that Danny was heading to the kitchen.

The boy spun into the doorway, awkwardly arranging his chair so his jutting cast extended partway into the room. His small face was contorted, pink with anger. "You always promised me that you'd never break a promise, but you did, so you broke two promises. It's not fair. You're not fair." Tears spurted right on cue. "Momma didn't ever break a promise, not ever. I hate you."

Jarod felt like he'd been gut-kicked by a rampaging bull.

"Mind your manners, child," Martha said. She spoke quietly, but with a no-nonsense edge that snapped the boy's mouth shut. "Don't be treating your father with disrespect. A boy who has no choice but to use his bottom for sitting oughtn't court himself a whipping."

Danny's eyes popped wider, then narrowed as he recognized the hollow threat. He'd never even been spanked, let alone whipped, and had no fear of either since he knew perfectly well that his father didn't believe in striking children.

Not that Danny escaped punishment for misbehavior. Jarod exercised discipline when necessary. At least, he tried to.

But he couldn't discipline his son for saying out loud what was already running through his own mind. Danny had every right to be angry, to feel betrayed.

"I'm sorry, son—" Jarod flinched as Danny wheeled backwards, pivoted the chair and rolled down the hallway. A moment later, the boy's bedroom door slammed.

Jarod closed his eyes, heard the snap of metal and realized he'd clenched his fist tightly enough to crush the beer can.

A warm hand patted his shoulder. "Don't pay it no mind. Guilt is a powerful weapon for getting one's own way. Children learn that quick enough."

Pinching the bridge of his nose, Jarod gathered his composure. He exhaled slowly, set the bent beer can on the counter and dropped his hand to his side.

"Danny has every right to feel angry and betrayed," he whispered. "A promise is a sacred oath."

"People break promises all the time. Things happen, circumstances change. 'Tis not the end of the world."

Jarod didn't respond. He couldn't. Martha couldn't know that but for a broken promise, Danny's mother would still be alive.

Chapter Two

"I hafta do all that? In only one week?" Danny shoved the assignment list aside, and rolled away from the dining room table with a disgruntled snort. "It's not fair. You're being really mean."

Susan smiled, moved the purring Claude off her class-studies binder. The big tomcat yawned, repositioned himself on a comfy stack of spelling lists while Susan studied the angry boy across from her. "I know it will be difficult. It's been several weeks since your surgery, and your class has moved ahead rather quickly. The school year will be over soon so you'll have all summer to catch up. By September your leg will be good as new, and you'll be ready to rejoin your classmates in the fourth grade!"

Danny grumbled, frowned, rolled his chair away from a kitchen table piled with textbooks and papers. "I shouldn't have to work so hard just because I fell off a stupid horse. It's not fair. It's not." He angled a contrite glance. "Besides, I always do okay in school."

"Hmm." Susan glanced at Danny's transcript, which reflected a student of average ability who frequently performed sub-par work. "Well, I don't think your grades thus far have been an accurate reflection of your ability." She laid down the transcript, regarded the sullen child quietly. "Schoolwork doesn't interest you much, does it?"

Danny rolled his eyes. "No-o-o." He drew out the word with exaggerated sarcasm. "Like, who cares about fractions and long division, and old wars where soldiers couldn't even shoot real guns. It's dumb. I don't care about that stuff."

"What do you care about, Danny?"

His brow hitched with suspicion, a manner chillingly familiar. For that instant, he looked just like his father...wary, vulnerable, secretly scared. "I dunno. Stuff."

"What kind of stuff?"

His gaze narrowed. He shrugged. "I like to draw sometimes."

"Drawing can be lots of fun. What things do you enjoy drawing the most?"

"I dunno."

"I'd like to see your work. Will you show it to me?"

The child shifted in his wheelchair, flinched at the effort. "There's a bulletin board in the kitchen, where Martha puts her grocery list and stuff. Dad hangs some of my pictures there, too."

"I'll make a point of checking them out." She hesitated, studied the child's pale complexion. "Are you in pain, Danny? I could ask Martha if it's time for your medication."

"Nah, it doesn't hurt none."

That was clearly untrue, although Susan thought it best not to press the issue. "How long will it be before you'll be able to walk with crutches?"

"I dunno. Dad says maybe a couple more weeks. It depends on what they see when they take X rays and stuff." The child brightened. "I got a steel bar in my leg now. I'm kinda like the bionic man, y'know?"

Susan laughed. "You like that idea, do you?"

"Yeah, it's like, way cool."

She'd learned from Danny's school records that the riding accident had shattered his thighbone so badly there was concern he might actually lose the leg. "You're a very brave young man, Danny. You've been through a frightening experience."

He shifted, glanced away. "Yeah, well...dumb horse."

"Accidents happen."

"It wasn't an accident. Thunder hated everybody." A glaze of pain veiled the child's eyes, an anguish that seemed more emotional than physical. "Nobody but Dad was supposed to ride him."

"If you weren't supposed to ride him, why did you?"

The question seemed to surprise Danny. "I wanted to."

"Do you always do everything you want to do?"

He blinked. "Yeah. Why shouldn't I?"

"Because there are usually reasons behind rules." She pointedly nodded at the massive cast extending from the boy's small foot to the apex of his thigh, where his jeans had been sheared off, sliced up the hip, and refastened with Velcro. ''And because when we break rules, we frequently hurt ourselves.''

The moment the words were out, Susan wished she could swallow them whole. Because they were too true. She of all people understood the unforeseen consequence of breaking rules.

Her hand automatically went to her belly, as if the gesture could protect the precious life stirring within. Choice wrought consequence. Sometimes the innocent suffered. But not this time. Not while there was breath in her body.

Susan was grimly determined that her child would not suffer the stigma of its mother's poor choices. This child would be nurtured and loved beyond measure.

''Rules are stupid,'' Danny announced suddenly. A defensive frown furrowed his small forehead in yet another uncomfortably familiar expression. ''Besides, Thunder was a really cool horse, a mustang that used to be wild. I took really good care of him. I gave him carrots every day and walked him out to the paddock for exercise. It's not my fault he was only half saddle-broke. Thunder was supposed to be *my* horse. It wasn't fair that I couldn't ride him. Dad rode him all the time.''

A hint of bitterness in the child's voice took her aback. ''Your father is no doubt a more experienced rider.''

''Big deal.''

''Why does that make you angry, Danny?''

''It doesn't. I don't care.''

''You sound like you care.''

''Well, I don't.'' He huffed, shifted, folded his arms like a shield across his heart. ''I don't care at all. I hate horses. I hate cows. I hate this ranch, and so did my mother.''

Stunned, Susan leaned back in the hardwood dining chair, buying a moment of time by stroking the purring cat sprawled on her assignment papers.

The boy's resentment toward his father was startling and disheartening. After all Susan was here to watch, observe and determine if Jarod Bodine was one of those precious few men who actually deserved the title of father, along with a coveted—and permanent— place in his child's life.

Part of her, the rational, intellectual part, understood that worthy or not, any man had a right to know he'd fathered a child. The other part of her, the part subjected to repeated paternal rejection, was determined not to subject yet another helpless human to the betrayal and abandonment she had suffered as a child.

In truth, Susan had initially presumed Jarod Bodine to be a good father. Everything she'd learned about him supported that, including his determination to provide his son with the best medical care, the best educational opportunity, the best of everything.

Of course, money wasn't a problem for Jarod, any more than it had been a problem for any Bodine in a county the family had practically owned for more decades than locals could count.

Susan had nonetheless been impressed by the methodical manner in which he'd gone about choosing tutor applicants. The fact that she'd managed to twist a few arms at the school board to place herself on the list was another matter entirely.

Not that she totally understood why she'd gotten the job. Initially she'd counted on their previous interaction to give her an edge with Jarod. She'd hoped that his initial interest in her would extend to her unexpected reappearance in his life.

Clearly, it hadn't. That had disappointed her but hadn't truly surprised her.

His son's anger with him did surprise her. And it disappointed her more than she cared to admit.

Susan's gaze slipped past the sulking youngster across the table to a mantel of framed photographs just beyond the open dining area. A woman with bright eyes and a thick mane of glossy brown hair smiled back. Danny's mother, no doubt, since those coffee-brown eyes bore a striking similarity to those of the child whose arms were now folded tightly across his scrawny little-boy chest.

"Your mother was a lovely woman," she said.

Danny blinked, automatically gazed toward the raft of photographs, lovingly arranged. A flicker of emotion darkened his expression.

"You must miss her terribly."

He frowned, shrugged, but he unfolded his arms, dropping his hands into his lap in a gesture of receptiveness. "I remember she always smelled really good. Her hair used to fall down and tickle my face when she tucked me in."

Susan studied Danny Bodine, wondering what features her own child might inherit. Would the baby share its brother's subtle chin dimple? The tousled shock of stick-straight hair? How about the adorable scatter of freckles that sprinkled his snubbed nose, or the hint of a cleft in his small chin? Danny was a striking child, although he bore more resemblance to the smiling woman whose photographs graced the mantel than to his father, a man of sharp angles and hard features whose appeal more aptly fit the realm of darkly dangerous than suavely debonair.

She wondered how Danny would react to having a baby brother or sister. She wondered how Jarod Bodine would react to his impending fatherhood. But most of all, Susan wondered if either of them would ever know about the tiny Bodine now growing in her womb.

Choices do indeed have consequence. Susan now faced the most crucial decision of her life. She would live with the consequence.

So would her child.

Spring was a volatile season, the clash between winter's deadly chill and the killing heat of summer. The morning had been clear, warm, with an azure sky that encircled the edge of the Montana plains like loving arms. By the time Susan emerged from the Bodine ranch house, the air snapped cold, and a blustery wind howled in from the north.

Pausing on the porch, she scanned an endless horizon blemished only by a few stoic plateaus in the distance. Breathtaking, she thought. Truly God's country, especially in comparison to the bustling suburbs of southern California where she'd been raised.

Everything in Montana reeked of agelessness, perfected by eons and fortunately unimproved by the hand of man. Even the few dwellings constructed in this beautiful wilderness meshed with the land, their timbers grayed with age, frayed by weather, yet dignified somehow, and as enduring as those who made their homes here.

Newness seemed out of place, like the smooth, clear

pine boards used to build a temporary wheelchair ramp at the edge of the ancient planking of the front porch.

Susan descended the ramp, stood on the rocky ground beside the porch noting the sturdiness of the ramp's construction. The fact that it had been built at all was telling, since it would only be needed for a few weeks, a convenience for an angry youngster whose needs, even temporary needs, were clearly considered a priority by someone.

Susan had a pretty good idea who that was.

"Is class over?"

She pivoted quickly enough to throw herself off balance. One hand reached for a rough-hewn baluster, the other absently went to her throat.

Jarod's presence shadowed the land, blocked the massive view with broad shoulders and a riveting countenance that could not be looked around or ignored.

"Yes. I'll be back on Friday." Susan gulped a breath, forced herself to lower both hands to her side. "If Danny has difficulty with the assignments I've given him, let me know. I'll increase my time with him."

A battered, wide-brimmed hat shadowed Jarod's face, but not enough that she couldn't see the harsh glint in his eye. "Three days a week is enough."

"Yes, it should be enough."

"It is."

Her skin was hot, her palms were clammy. She twisted her hands together, hoped her discomfort wasn't obvious. "I haven't had the chance to thank you for giving me the job."

"Don't bother." He shifted his stance, lifted his hat long enough to wipe his brow with his forearm, then replaced the headgear without looking in her direction. "You're here because Danny wants you here."

"I suspected as much. Danny usually gets what he wants, doesn't he?"

Jarod continued to gaze past her, as if she didn't exist. "Don't judge my son. You know nothing about the difficulties he's had to deal with in his life."

It might have been an appropriate moment to comment that it wasn't his son she was judging. Instead, she took his cue, turned away from him, gazing across the ranch.

A rutted road led up toward a crisscross of split-rail fences and a rectangular building she knew to be the stables.

Closer to the house an old barn stood proudly, its weathered gray siding immaculately maintained. Outside it, a few hay bales were stacked in the front-loader of a midsize tractor.

A rusty plow had been planted in the earth, and a scatter of hearty petunias peeked from the cool soil around it. There was an untidiness to the small garden, as if whatever grew was mere happenstance, an emergence of seeds sown by last year's planting rather than a garden that had been lovingly tended. Still, the old plow would be wrapped in color by midsummer. Whoever had prepared the original planting had done so with loving care, and an artistic eye for the eventual result.

She returned her attention to Jarod. "You're right, I shouldn't judge your son, because I don't know enough about the difficulties he has had to deal with in his young life. I would like to know, however."

"It's not your business."

''The better I understand Danny, the more help I can be.''

''You're not here to help him. You're here to educate him.'' The comment was issued quietly, without rancor.

''One is the natural outcome of the other.'' Susan moistened her lips, turned her gaze and found herself staring directly into the same cool hazel eyes that had so utterly charmed her just a few scant months ago. For the briefest of moments, she saw a glimpse of question, a hint of vulnerability.

Then he blinked, and it was gone. ''I apologize if I sounded hostile.''

''You didn't sound hostile. You sounded cynical.''

He smiled, ever so slightly. ''Can you blame me?''

She felt her own lips curve in response. ''Under the circumstances, no, I can't blame you. I'm sure your first instinct was that I had chased you down to take up where we left off....'' Her voice trailed off as he turned his head to the side, but not quite far enough that she couldn't see the color rise up his throat. ''Are you blushing?''

''Of course not,'' he growled, although a distinct crimson stain crept along his jawline.

''Yes, you are. That's adorable.''

He shifted, toed a rock with his boot, and issued a gruff snort. ''Of all the things I do not want to be, adorable pretty much tops the list.''

''I just call 'em like I see 'em.'' Her grin faded. ''Are you really that embarrassed about what happened between us? If you are, perhaps we should talk about it.''

His eyes widened, then narrowed. He glanced up at the house, his gaze bouncing from the front door to each of the small, mullioned windows, then he scooped her elbow into his palm and ushered her toward her car, which was parked near the barn. "If you insist on discussing this, we will do so once, and only once. Then I never want to hear it mentioned again."

. Offended, she pulled her arm from his grasp, pivoted to face him. "Oh, hail, Exalted One. Forgive me for providing the impression that I enjoy being ordered about."

To her surprise, he burst into rich, mellow laughter. "You're right. I apologize. Again."

Miffed, but with her righteous indignation thwarted, Susan took pains to smooth foolishly the front of her bulky-knit sweater. She turned her head, allowing the wind to whip her hair out of her face.

"It happened," she said simply. "No amount of pretending otherwise is helpful. We both agreed that neither of us was proficient in the art of one-night stands, but we presumed the appropriate protocol was to exchange phone numbers, promise to call, then politely to disappear, never to be seen or heard from again."

When he didn't reply immediately, she angled a glance, saw that his smile was a little sad, slightly nostalgic. "I remember. I also recall that we jointly agreed to dispense with the phone-number exchange."

It hadn't exactly been a joint agreement.

The sex had been great. Too great, actually. It was the aftermath that had left them shuffling, nervous, straining for the proper etiquette. They'd both been tentative, awkward...rather like they were now.

An image flickered into her mind, a vision of two nervous people in a snowy motel parking lot, alternately gazing into the star-studded sky and sneaking glances at each other. He had been poignantly chivalrous, wrapping his leather jacket around her shoulders to protect her from the frigid wind. When she'd finally slipped into her vehicle, he'd carefully cleaned the new snow and ice from her windshield and lingered at the driver's side for several minutes after she'd returned his jacket to him.

She'd started the car engine, and they'd stared at each other until her breath frosted the glass. For all Susan knew, he'd still been standing there after she'd put the car into gear and driven into the cold, dark night.

Now silence stretched between them again, and a cold wind whistled through a rustling stand of poplars behind the barn. She studied Jarod's faraway expression, wondered if he, too, was remembering the brief moments of magic they had shared.

He closed his eyes, massaged them with his fingertips. "I know I told you before that I wasn't in the habit of picking up strange women in bars—"

"Yes, you told me." She swallowed, studied her feet. "Just as I told you that I wasn't in the habit of being picked up by strange men in bars."

"It wasn't really a bar."

"No, it was technically a pub."

"They served great steaks there."

"The best. That's why I went."

"Me, too. I'd been driving back from Billings, and was starving...." His voice trailed off. A moment later, he cleared his throat. "We both spent considerable time that night justifying ourselves, didn't we?"

"Yes." It was a whisper. "Strangers in the night. That would make a lovely song title, don't you think?"

He responded with a thin smile. "It's been done."

"Ah. Just our luck." She licked her lips, grasped the car door handle. "I gave Danny a list of assignments in case you want to review them. He may need some encouragement, since he's not feeling very well and doesn't appear to enjoy his schoolwork under the best of circumstance. Also—"

She gasped as he touched her arm.

He immediately pulled his hand back, jammed it in the pocket of an oversized jacket lined with sheepskin. "I just wanted to say…" He swallowed, kicked a rock. "I just wanted to tell you that I…"

Susan waited a moment.

He exhaled all at once. "Oh, hell."

"I know." Oddly enough, she did know. There wasn't anything to say, yet words, feelings, emotions, all clogged in her throat as if desperate to escape. "I'll see you on Friday."

"Right. Friday."

Jarod stepped back, watching Susan's vehicle wind down the dirt drive, and disappear from view. He sighed, tugged his hat down. "You can come out now, Samuel."

After a moment, the barn door creaked. A thin, craggy-faced man with bowed legs and a chin stubbled with gray whiskers emerged. He wore no jacket, only a plaid flannel shirt as protection against the frigid wind.

Samuel sniffed to the west, spit on the ground, and wiped his mouth with his shirtsleeve. "Need me some help hoisting those squeeze chutes into the truck bed."

Jarod gazed out over the land his great-grandfather had homesteaded nearly a century ago. "How much did you hear?"

"I heard some, I guess. The old barn ain't exactly soundproof."

"Especially when you've got an ear pressed over a knothole."

"I was working. Ain't my fault your grand-pappy used cheap timber to build hisself a danged barn." Samuel made a noise low in his throat, coughed, then added, "But since you asked my opinion—"

"I didn't ask your opinion."

"You were going to. Just saving a bit of time, is all, cutting straight to the chase."

Jarod shot him a look. "It would be nice if you'd leave me the impression, no matter how erroneous it might be, that I'm actually in charge around here."

"You're the boss, and that's a fact."

"Thank you." Jarod waited a moment. "Well?"

"Well what, boss man?"

"Your opinion. What is it?"

"Oh, I wouldn't want to step on your polished, boss-in-charge toes."

"Dammit, Samuel—"

"The lady has more in mind than tutoring your boy." Samuel scraped his chin with his knuckles, twisted his thin lips. "Something's eating at her, that's for sure. Don't know what."

"Maybe she just finds me irresistibly attractive."

"Nah, that ain't it."

Jarod's ego quivered. "It's not impossible, you know."

"Oh, I ain't saying she don't find you appealing. Maybe she does. Can't say for certain."

"You pride yourself on having instincts honed to the point of psychic, and you can't say for certain?"

"Her signals are all tangled up. Caught me a

glimpse through that old knothole, I did, and danged if she didn't slip you a glance when you wasn't looking that practically tore them dungarees right off your behind.''

"Really?" The image pleased him, although he couldn't for the life of him explain why. The last thing he needed in his life was the complication of a relationship, even one built solely on physical attraction rather than emotional depth.

Before Jarod's ego had a chance to puff, Samuel stuck a pin in it.

"Two seconds later," the older man opined, "she's got this disgusted look, kinda like she'd just kissed a badger square on the lips." He shrugged one scrawny shoulder. "Like I said, her eyes got something serious going on in them, but I can't quite figure what it is."

A chill slipped down Jarod's spine. His daddy would have said that meant someone had walked over his grave.

"I'll keep my distance."

"No, you won't." Samuel spat on the ground again. "I saw more through that old knothole than her looking at you. I saw you looking back." He wiped his puckered mouth, squinted up into the wind. "Gonna be a gully-washer tonight. We best get those chutes set up before the mud's too deep for the truck."

With that, Samuel sauntered back into the barn, leaving Jarod standing alone in the wind, gaping and panic-stricken. The chill returned, grasping his spine like frigid fingers. Someone wasn't just walking over his grave. Someone was digging it.

And in the deepest, most secret place in his mind, he saw himself with a shovel in his hand.

Chapter Three

Rain pounded the shingled roof, pummeling the ranch-house windows like a thousand tiny fists.

Dropping his fork on his plate, Danny rolled away from the dinner table. "How come you don't like Miss Mitchell, Dad? She's really cool."

Startled, Jarod bought himself a moment of thought by using his napkin. A dozen replies spurted through his mind, only to be discarded. He finally settled on one that was true enough to keep his palms from sweating or otherwise revealing the turmoil eating him up inside.

He cleared his throat, laid the napkin beside his half-eaten meal. "I don't know her well enough to dislike her."

"So how come you look at her that way?"

"What way?"

"You know, like you think she's gonna steal Momma's silverware or something."

That startled him. "I certainly don't think she's going to steal any silverware." Jarod coughed, bought a few more precious seconds by taking a sip of water. "What's really important is what you think of Miss Mitchell."

"I like her."

"I figured that much." He set the glass down, regarded his son with a father's perception. "What is it about her that you like so much? Besides her 'smiley eyes,' that is."

Martha had relayed a few eavesdropped tidbits about the tutorial sessions, enough for Jarod to learn that despite the boy's enthusiasm for his new teacher, he'd nonetheless grumbled through his lessons in typical Danny fashion. What had truly interested Jarod was Martha's comment about how much laughter punctuated those same lessons. Danny hadn't laughed much lately, and certainly hadn't told Jarod any of the corny jokes Martha had mentioned overhearing him tell Miss Mitchell.

Then again, Jarod wasn't known for a sterling sense of humor. He'd always been serious about life. Perhaps too serious.

"Martha tells me that you and Miss Mitchell laugh a lot during your sessions."

"She's always making jokes and stuff. Like she told me that the reason George Washington chopped down that cherry tree was because he needed the wood for his teeth!" Danny's grin faded with his father's blank stare. "It's a joke, Dad."

"Oh." Jarod managed an appreciative smile that didn't fool his son for a minute.

"You don't get it, do you?"

"Ah, well…so that's why you like Miss Mitchell, because she tells good jokes?"

"Yeah, kinda." Danny shrugged. "She's fun to be with because she's the only grown-up I ever met who can scream louder than me."

Jarod laughed. The reminder of a pink-faced woman gyrating wildly to dislodge a rodent from beneath her skirt really was humorous, although at the time he'd been too stunned by the identity of the woman in question to appreciate it. "I didn't realize a loud shriek was an educational requisite. I'll keep that in mind."

"Miss Mitchell likes cats, too. Even after the mouse thing, she petted Claude and made him purr and stuff. And she doesn't wrinkle her nose when the wind blows from the stables, like that foggy old prune that came before her did. You know what else?" A glitter of happiness shone in the youngster's bright eyes as he blurted the answer. "Miss Mitchell said that if I work real hard on my studies, she'll take me to watch my friends play summer-league baseball. Isn't that too cool?"

Apparently Jarod's expression was one of shocked disbelief, because the boy quickly added, "But only if it's okay with the doctor. And you."

The last two words were clearly an afterthought.

When Jarod didn't immediately reply, Danny's brows crinkled anxiously. The child had nice brows, neat and well-arched, unlike the horizontal tangle shading Jarod's own eyes.

"It is okay, isn't it, Dad? I mean, you wouldn't say I can't go, would you?"

Struggling with a smile that seemed to crack his face like dry leather, Jarod leaned back in his chair, casually propped an ankle on his knee. "We'll have to wait and see how you're feeling when the time comes, son. It seems to me that you'd be pretty sad watching all your friends play ball when you can't join them this year. I know how much you loved being on the team."

Danny's smile faded. He balled his small fists, folded his arms across his chest. "It's better than staying here. Anything is better than staying here."

A lump of pure fear settled into the pit of Jarod's stomach. He'd known his son was lonely. He just hadn't realized how lonely. And how isolated.

It was heartbreaking watching a boy who had been a whirlwind of activity suddenly thrust into forced immobility and constant pain. The Claude-and-mouse mishap was probably the most exciting thing Danny had seen since the accident that had left him permanently scarred, both physically and emotionally.

Jarod would have given his own life to take back that moment in time, and one other moment as well. If not for his own obsession with a stallion that should never have been saddle-broke in the first place, Danny would still be a happy, active little boy.

And if not for his obsession with land reddened by the blood of generations, Danny's mother would still be alive.

Unable to swallow the lump in his throat, Jarod managed to speak around it. "Are you up to a game of Monopoly tonight? It won't take me long to clean up the kitchen, and—" A thump on the front door startled him.

Danny heard it too. "What was that?"

Jarod pushed away from the table and stood.

''Maybe the cat wants in. The storm is really howling out there.''

''Claude's asleep in my bedroom,'' Danny said, wheeling from the dining room to the living area. ''I brought him in when it started to rain, right after Miss Mitchell left.''

Jarod heard two more weak thumps as he strode toward the door, opened it—and was stunned by what he saw.

There she stood, wet and shivering, an apologetic expression in eyes narrowed against the wind-blown rain. ''I know I'm th-the last person on earth you want to s-see right now...'' she sneezed, gasped, shivered so hard Jarod feared her chattering teeth might crack ''...but could I please use your phone to c-call a cab?''

Jarod pushed open the screen door, slipped an arm around her soggy shoulders and pulled her inside. She swayed on her feet, sneezed again, her wet hair flung forward and stuck as if glued to her pale cheeks.

She looked like the proverbial drowned rat, a point not lost on Danny, whose mood instantly brightened at yet another exciting mishap surrounding the mishap-prone Miss Mitchell. ''You're a real mess,'' the boy said happily. ''Did you fall into the creek or something?''

She managed a thin smile. ''Not exactly.''

''Flash flood?'' Jarod asked.

She nodded. ''I missed the turn. Rain on the windshield...'' she paused, shivered, ''...couldn't see. Road washed out. Mud everywhere. My car is stuck up to the hubcaps in m-muck.''

Jarod stripped off her soaked jacket, flung it aside. Her waterlogged sweater drooped halfway to her knees. "We'll drag it out with the tractor after the storm passes."

Her eyes widened. "I don't want to bother you. I'll just call a tow truck—"

"Tow trucks don't come this far out." Jarod gritted his teeth, reminded yet again that the isolation he cherished came with a price. "As for getting a cab, you'd have a better chance of sprouting wings to fly out."

"I—I was afraid of that." She sneezed twice, shivered, hitched her shoulder bag and glanced at the telephone on an end table beside the garishly flowered sofa. "I'm l-late for a PTA meeting. I should c-call—"

"The phone is out." Jarod slipped her handbag off her shoulder, hung it on a coat hook. "The phones always go out during a storm. Part of the charm of living in the wilderness."

"Oh." She sneezed again, gasped for breath, cast a yearning glance at the crackling fire blazing across the room. The small gas-fed flame was more for atmosphere than an efficient heating source. Since wood was as scarce as trees in eastern Montana, most rural homes relied on propane to fuel furnaces and for cooking. "The fire is lovely. Perhaps I could warm up?"

"Of course. Sorry." He ushered her across the room, noting her stiff movements and unsteady gait. Not a surprise, since it was barely forty degrees outside. She must be half-frozen. "How long have you been out in that weather?"

"I don't know."

She sighed, held her hands up in front of the fire. A moan of pleasure slipped from her throat, a sound familiar enough to flash an erotic memory from the night they'd spent together. His groin tightened in response. He instantly turned away, disgusted with himself.

"A couple of hours," she murmured. "It was like walking the wrong way in a frigid wind tunnel. Three steps forward, two steps back." She sighed again, flipped her hair forward and finger-combed it in the heat radiating from the small, flickering gas fire. "I was utterly lost. If I hadn't spotted your house lights up on this ridge, I'd still be huddled under a bush waiting to drown."

"That is so cool!" Danny was fried with excitement. "I mean, like, you almost died and stuff. You could write a book, huh?"

She chuckled, a mellow sound that did peculiar things to Jarod's insides. Danny was right, he noted. Miss Mitchell did have smiley eyes.

"I don't know about the book part." She slicked her wet hair back, then flexed her white fingers in front of the fire. "I doubt anyone would be interested in reading about a too-dumb-to-live city slicker who can't tell north from south without a compass and drives dirt roads in a rainstorm."

"I would," Danny assured her.

She laughed again, sending a new army of goose bumps marching down Jarod's spine. "I think I love you," she told Danny.

The boy beamed.

Still smiling, Susan stretched her soggy sweater toward the fireplace in a futile attempt to dry it. "I'm dripping all over your lovely hardwood floors. I'm so sorry."

"These floors have seen worse." Jarod knew he sounded gruff. He couldn't help himself. Gruff was an excellent protective measure to shield a man's real feelings. His dad had taught him that. His dad had always been right. Always.

So why did the wounded look in her eyes affect him like a body blow?

Jarod spun on his booted heel, marched out of the room. A moment later he returned with the useless terrycloth bathrobe his mother-in-law had sent him as a Christmas gift nearly a decade earlier. It had never been worn. He gave it a lazy toss, not trusting himself to get any closer to the woman whose presence evoked so many erotic thoughts.

Susan awkwardly caught the rumpled garment, then questioned him with her eyes.

"Put it on," he said through clenched teeth. Damn, a woman had no right to look that good soaking wet. No right at all. "Bathroom is down the hall, clothes dryer is in the laundry room, through the kitchen."

"Th-thank you."

He suspected her stammer now had less to do with being cold than her shock at his sharp tone. "The guest room is the first door on your left. I'll get some clean sheets."

That got her attention. "Guest room? Oh, no, really, that's not necessary."

Clenching his fists at his side, he forced himself to look at her. Her eyes were huge, her face pale, her sultry lips parted just far enough to make a man want to taste them. Especially a man who knew exactly how delectably sweet those lips truly were.

He sucked a breath, held it, exhaled all at once. "That's up to you. You can sleep on the sofa, curl up on the floor, or just stand in front of the fire all night. Makes no difference to me. I just figured you might prefer some privacy."

She flushed, as if recalling that privacy was something she hadn't been particularly concerned about the first time they'd met. "I don't want to put you out, that's all."

"Lady, you already have."

And with that, Jarod stomped out of the room, painfully aware that he'd just been incredibly rude to a woman who didn't deserve it. Even worse, he'd done it in front of his son.

The steaming shower streamed over her chilled body like manna from heaven. When the water turned tepid, she realized that she'd selfishly used every drop of hot water in the house, and regretfully stepped out to dry herself with a clean, but well-used towel. It was a blue towel, which had been hanging beside a flowered gold-and-brown towel, which in turn was next to a pink washcloth, a yellow washcloth and a green face towel.

Color coordination apparently didn't rank high on the decorator scale for isolated ranch houses. Susan had noticed that the living area was also creatively eclectic, with a variety of colors and textures on furniture, mostly well-used and heavily worn. There were unique items of decor on the walls—a twist of wire with a silk rose wound around a tintype photograph; a rusted chain entwined with hand-tatted lace; an old funnel hung by a piece of carpet twine and stuffed with old railroad tickets. Window treatments were little more than drapes of vivid cloth twisted into odd knots, more like hairbows for windows than serviceable draperies.

The guest room had been painted a brilliant shade of yellow, so bright that turning on a lamp was akin to turning on sunshine. An expensive sewing machine was in the corner, neatly tucked into its own cherry-wood cabinet. The closet was filled with dusty bolts of cloth that clearly hadn't been disturbed for many years.

Despite a peculiar avant garde decor, the entire home was tidy enough, although Susan suspected Martha was responsible for the cleanliness.

Susan liked Martha, found her no-nonsense approach to her duties refreshingly logical. Although the woman seemed reluctant to indulge in trivial conversation, her perceptive gaze followed Danny's every move with quiet acuity. Susan had noticed that Martha positioned herself in the kitchen during Danny's lessons and appeared to be listening to every word. Susan wondered if she reported back to Jarod.

Jarod.

On cue, Susan removed the oversized bathrobe he'd given her from a hook on the bathroom door. She held it up, stunned by the sheer size of the garment. And even more stunned to realize that it was probably too small for the man who owned it. At least, it was probably too small in the shoulders. Susan had never seen a man with shoulders bigger than Jarod Bodine's.

To be fair, she realized that Jarod had to have big shoulders. How else could he support that huge chip he carried on them?

She issued a snort, slipped on the robe and promptly watched her hands and most of her legs disappear from view. She rolled up the sleeves, tied the sash. A pale scent of mothballs wafted up. Clearly this wasn't a garment he wore often, if ever.

Probably because the shoulders were too small.

She sighed, propped her hip against an old-fashioned washbasin, and found herself surprisingly disappointed that there was no trace of Jarod's scent on the robe.

She remembered his scent, poignantly and intimately. A night that had begun as a step toward emotional independence had ended up in the most passionate experience of her entire life. The memory still gave her goose bumps.

What a dichotomy he was. When Susan had first seen him watching her from across the crowded pub, she'd chalked him up as just another bar-hugging cowboy on a weekly prowl for female company. A few moments of conversation and a glimpse into his sad eyes had convinced her otherwise and had melted what little was left of her own resistance.

They had been like souls drawn together by an intrinsic need for comfort. There had been something unique about him, a sad gentleness and tender strength that had touched a chord deep in her soul, allowed her to lower her guard. Intimacy with strangers was not her normal behavior. For some odd reason that she'd yet to decipher, Jarod hadn't seemed like a stranger. She'd felt as if she had known him forever.

Clearly it had all been a ruse, the deficient meanderings of a broken heart and a beer-drugged mind. The real Jarod Bodine was cranky, rude, a man who possessed none of the qualities she'd initially perceived in him.

A man who possessed none of the qualities necessary to be a viable part of her child's life.

She shuddered, tightened the robe belt over the tiny bulge of her belly. This wasn't the first time a man had disappointed her. But it was damn well going to be the last.

Grim and determined, she yanked open the bathroom door, marched into the narrow hall and immediately bounced off a large, unyielding male chest.

Jarod steadied her, releasing his grip on her shoulders as she deliberately stepped away. She regarded him warily for a moment, then avoided his gaze. "I used all the hot water."

"It's there to be used."

"I just wanted to warn you that you'd have to take a cold shower, that's all."

"No worse than I deserve."

A quiver of remorse in his voice drew her gaze like a magnet. To her surprise, the same regret was reflected in his eyes.

"I owe you another apology. With this much practice, I should be getting good at it."

Susan narrowed her gaze. "What are you sorry for this time? Besides the fact that chivalry dictates you not throw a woman you clearly despise into the jaws of a raging storm, no matter how tempted you are to do exactly that."

He blinked, acquiesced with the tip of his head. "I deserved that, I suppose. I don't despise you, Susan. Not even close." He sighed, raked his hair with his fingers. "I'd like to explain my behavior, but I'm not sure I can. I guess it's just that seeing you again has brought back...memories."

A shiver slipped down her spine. "Believe it or not, I understand what you mean."

He glanced down the hallway, to a closed door at the end of the narrow, hardwood corridor. Danny's room, Susan suspected, but didn't bother to ask, since Jarod had slipped a palm under her elbow and was ushering her into the living area.

When they were at the farthest possible point from that bedroom off the hallway, Jarod released her, shuffled his feet, and rubbed the back of his neck. He spoke very quietly, obviously in deference to the possibility of prying ears on the other side of the house. ''I have to admit that I've thought about that night a lot over the past few weeks.''

Susan's heart leaped, fluttered, then began to pound like the proverbial jackhammer. She, too, had thought about the night in question, thought about it a lot. Some nights she couldn't seem to think about anything else. ''Have you?''

''Actually, it's probably good that we had an opportunity to see each other again.''

''Is it?'' Her voice sounded breathless, saccharine, too sweetly deferential for a woman who prided herself on self-reliance in the extreme.

Jarod didn't seem to notice. He simply nodded. ''I just wanted you to know…'' His voice trailed off. He coughed, cleared his throat.

''Yes?''

Those broad shoulders slumped slightly. ''It seems like all I do is apologize to you for my behavior, so you probably don't need to hear it again. Still, I want you to know how deeply I regret what happened that night.''

The hope that had spiraled without permission was instantly and cruelly dashed. A pain caught in her chest, stunning her with its intensity. It served her right. Truthfully, she hadn't expected any better. She just wished that she had as much control over her heart as she did over her rational mind.

With every ounce of dignity she could muster, she

squared her shoulders, lifted her chin. "You could not possibly regret it as much as I do, Mr. Bodine."

Then she spun on her bare heel, strode directly into the guest room, closed the door and wept.

The scream awakened her, a wrenching shriek of agony that ripped through her very soul.

Susan leaped from the bed, terrified, confused, befuddled with sleep. For a moment, she didn't recognize where she was. Moonlight shone through an unfamiliar window, then darkened behind a passing cloud. Outside, the storm had passed. Inside, it was just beginning.

Another scream tore through the darkness, then merged into the keening wail of a wounded soul. Susan stumbled forward, stubbed her foot on a dresser hidden in shadows. As she fumbled for the doorknob, she heard footsteps on the hardwood floor. Fast steps and heavy.

By the time she emerged into the hallway, the screams had subsided into wrenching sobs. She followed the sounds to the room at the end of the hallway. The door was open now. She peeked inside and saw movement. Shadows, one large and one small. Before her eyes accustomed themselves to the darkness, the moon peeked through the window, illuminating the area enough for her to recognize the man seated on the bed, comforting the sobbing child.

"It's okay," Jarod was whispering. "It was only a bad dream, that's all."

"Th-Thunder—" Danny hiccuped, shuddered out loud. "He chased me. His eyes were all red and smoke came out of his nose, and...and...and he wanted to kill me dead."

"Shh, son, nothing is going to hurt you."

"Did you shoot him, Dad? Did you kill him?" The boy's voice quivered with fear, shook with rage. "Samuel said you made sure that Thunder would never hurt anybody again."

Jarod paused, spoke with a caution that Susan recognized as evasive. "Samuel was right, son. You're safe now. Thunder can't hurt you any more."

"Horses are dumb, stupid, mean animals. They all deserve to die." The boy broke down in a fresh burst of sobs.

The shadows merged, as if the father had gathered the crying child in his arms. "It's okay to be angry, son."

Jarod murmured other words of comfort, but Susan couldn't hear them. She could, however, hear gentle understanding in his voice, see love expressed by the tender movement of his silhouetted form.

"Stay with me, Daddy," Danny sobbed. "Please, don't go away."

"I'll never leave you, son. Never in a thousand, million years."

Danny sniffed, allowed his father to lower him back onto the pillows. "Promise?"

"I promise." Jarod tucked the bedclothes around his son, taking care to cover the immobile leg with exquisite gentleness. "Go back to sleep now. If any more red-eyed stallions show up, I'll be right here to chase them away."

Susan backed away, feeling as if she was intruding on a private moment. Still, she was deeply touched by what she'd seen, and by what she'd heard.

I'll never leave you…never in a thousand, million years.

What a wonder, she thought, a father who promised he would never, ever leave. Even more of a wonder was that she knew in her heart that it was true. Jarod would never abandon his child. Or his children.

At that moment, Susan realized that in spite of his gruffness, in spite of intense disappointment that he regretted a moment of passion that she secretly cherished, Jarod Bodine had passed the first test of fatherhood.

Perhaps he would prove worthy after all.

Chapter Four

Jarod was unhooking the front of the car bumper from the tow chain when he heard the screen door creak open. He didn't have to turn around to know that Susan was standing on the porch watching him. Her gaze affected him as tangibly as a touch, a silky warmth slipping down his spine.

It unnerved him.

He heard her light footsteps on the porch planks, noted a slight change in vibration as she descended the newly constructed ramp. A lifetime of bonding with the land itself had honed Jarod's senses to rapier sharpness. Perhaps that was why he could so acutely feel every nuance of her presence.

Perhaps that's why he'd lain awake last night, inhaling the subtle scent of her body even though she was sleeping in another room.

The delicate crunch of pebbles alerted him to her

progress. She was standing a few feet away now, close enough for her to notice that the tow chain was dangling from his hand. So much for the pretense that he was absorbed in a task he'd already completed several minutes ago. He had no excuse not to turn around.

No excuse except the fear of actually looking into a pair of eyes that affected him in ways he couldn't explain.

He heard the soft swish of her breath, knew before she uttered the first word that she was going to speak.

"Thank you." Her voice was a whisper, a nervous quiver that shook him to the bone. "I don't know what I would have done if you and Samuel hadn't retrieved my car for me. I know what a terrible imposition it was."

Jarod straightened as if totally unaffected by her presence, and absently tossed the rusty chain over the tractor's roll guard. "No problem."

"It wasted nearly two hours of your morning."

"We would have scouted the road to make sure it was passable anyway. There are a few other ranches in the area. They don't have the equipment to scrape a washout, or shore up a flooding creek bed. We do." He pushed the brim of his hat back, squinted at the clouds settled along the east horizon. "The storm has passed now. That's the thing about weather out here. If you don't like it, wait an hour. It'll change."

"Yes, I've heard that."

There was a smile in her voice. It annoyed him to notice. He noticed too damned much about Susan Mitchell, his attention diverted by every nuance of her sensually husky voice, the sparkle in grass-green eyes that were oddly tilted on the outer edges, giving her a sensual, exotic appeal, and that alluring little dimple that revealed itself not with a smile, but with a pensive pursing of lips lush enough that a man would sell his soul for a taste.

"I've lived in Montana nearly two years," she murmured. "It still surprises me."

"The land has its secrets. Too many for any mortal to learn in a single lifetime."

"Too bad a single lifetime is all any of us has."

"Maybe."

She paused a beat. "Some believe we live many lifetimes."

"Yes, some believe that."

"Do you?"

"I never gave it much thought." He tugged his hat down, planted a boot on the back of the tractor, stubbornly refusing to turn and look at her. "No sense wondering about things you can't change or control."

"Control is important to you, isn't it?"

"Only when I lose it." He planted both feet on the ground, made a point of studying the knobby tractor tires as if he actually cared about the clots of mud stuck between fat treads. "The ranch road has been scraped to hardpan, no mud problems there. You shouldn't have any trouble finding your way out. Just don't make any turns until you hit the gravel, then bear right until you see a paved feeder road. That leads to the interstate."

A muffled scuff of light shoes on hard dirt announced that she'd stepped closer to him. Her essence surrounded him, unique and untainted by perfumes or artificial fragrance beyond a subtle scent of soap. "What happened to Thunder?"

Stunned, Jarod spun around and saw the honest question reflected in her eyes. Her face was freshly scrubbed, radiant without a hint of makeup. A light blush of color tinted an ivory complexion with an appealing sprinkle of golden freckles that weren't visible when she used whatever it was women used to conceal such things. Most females looked better with a little cosmetic enhancement. This one was a breathtaking exception.

"I didn't mean to pry," she said quickly. She glanced away as if misreading his silence as an objection to her question. "I heard Danny cry out last night and went to see if I could help him. You were already there, of course."

Jarod would have responded if he could have thought of something to say.

Susan shifted, smoothed her sweater in a gesture he'd come to realize was one of deliberate distraction, then shaded her eyes with her hand, pivoting just enough that the ruffled hem of her skirt whipped around her ankles. "Does Danny have nightmares like that often?"

Jarod yanked his gaze from its wanderings, focused on her face. She was staring toward the horizon, but he doubted she was actually seeing anything beyond the image of a screaming child, terrified by equine demons and the ghosts of his own horrible fear. "He has nightmares sometimes. All kids do."

"Danny's nightmares seemed more intense than most." She lowered her hand, tilted her face toward him. "It's to be expected, I suppose. He's been through a harrowing and traumatic experience."

"He'll be okay."

"Yes, he'll recover, but I doubt he'll ever be quite the same. He's learned that he's not immortal. That's a terrifying lesson for a young child." Susan glanced up toward the stables, seeming to study the crisscrossing fences behind which a half-dozen animals frolicked and grazed. "When I was ten, my mother accidentally ran a stop sign while we were driving back from the grocery store. A pickup truck broadsided our car. Two of my fingers were broken, and I had to have stitches in my scalp. To this day, the sight of a pickup truck on the road makes me nervous."

The story was powerful, enough on target for Jarod to understand the parallel she was forming with Danny's fear. The personal revelation unnerved him enough to make him pretend he didn't understand. He nodded toward his own shiny pickup truck, a powerful model with enough muscle to climb a canyon wall pulling a trailer loaded with fat steers. "If you don't like pickup trucks, you sure picked the wrong state to live in."

She laughed. "True. I suspect there are more trucks in Montana than there are people to drive them. The point of my story is that my fear of pickup trucks was irrational, since the accident was my mother's fault."

Jarod understood her point. He simply didn't want to acknowledge it and wasn't certain why he felt that way. "All very interesting, I'm sure."

Her sigh probably wasn't meant to signal impatience, although Jarod took it as such. "Perhaps that was a poor comparison," she said. "What I'm trying to say is that Danny's fear of horses, irrational though it may be, isn't something he can necessarily control. Nor can you."

"I'm not trying to control anything."

"Aren't you? Look around." She gestured with her hand, encompassing the flat, treeless vistas beyond the house where cattle dotted the distant prairie, and horses foraged in fenced paddocks beside the massive stable building only a few hundred yards from the house. "Horses are a huge part of your lifestyle out here. Think about it, the terror Danny must feel just looking out the window. The sights, the sounds, the smells…everything that terrifies him is just outside the door. Yet he has no choice but to be terrified of the animal that threw him, because to lay the blame where it truly belongs, on his own willful behavior, would require him to be terrified of something he can't ever escape, even for a moment. Himself.''

Every muscle in Jarod's body tightened. "Thank you, Sigmund Freud.''

She massaged her forehead, then folded her arms. "I'm sorry. I know this is none of my business—''

"You're right. It isn't.''

"But Danny is my pupil, so I do have a vested interest in his emotional health.''

Jarod stared at her. "And I don't? He's my son, for God's sake. What the hell gives you the right to cross-examine me about raising my own child?''

Every trace of color drained from her face. An expression of pure agony flashed through her eyes, an expression that sent a wave of sheer terror down Jarod's spine. For the life of him, he didn't know why.

"Forgive me," she whispered. "I…I had absolutely no right to imply you were unconcerned about Danny's fears, especially after the way you comforted him last night. It's just that—'' She bit off the words as if they'd suddenly tasted foul. Conflict warred in her eyes, then slipped into sad resignation as she repeated her original question. "So what happened to Thunder?''

Jarod yanked his hat down, squinted into the breeze.

"I've got work to do. Samuel will lead you out, if you're worried about getting lost again."

"Did you shoot him?"

Jarod jerked to a stop, looked over his shoulder.

"It's a simple question. Did you kill the horse that threw your son or didn't you?"

"No, I didn't."

A flicker of relief passed through her eyes. "Why didn't you tell Danny that?"

"Because as you so astutely pointed out, Danny needs something tangible to hang his fear and anger on. That horse is the obvious choice. He needs to know that it can't hurt him any more."

"Where is the animal now?"

"On a ranch in Colorado, in the care of a friend who knows more about wild mustangs than anyone."

She considered that. "I think you should tell Danny."

"Why, so he can have more nightmares about the damned thing galloping five hundred miles just to break into his bedroom and finish the job?"

"No," she said quietly. "To alleviate his terror that he was responsible for the death of an animal that he secretly loved. I think he can live with the nightmares, Jarod. I don't think he can live with the guilt."

Jarod felt like he'd been gut-kicked.

Guilt.

The silent assassin. Fearsome. Predatory. Stalker of mind shadows, killer of souls.

Jarod knew guilt, had gazed into its bogeyman eyes, felt its sharp teeth pierce the soft flesh of his heart. Guilt had consumed him, devoured him whole. It haunted him still, an invisible specter of misery hovering just out of reach.

Yes, Jarod knew guilt, understood it on the most intimate of levels. It was a part of him now, intrinsically merged into his spirit and his soul. Guilt had claimed him as its own.

He would not allow it to claim his son.

"Hurry up, slowpoke! Growing season will be over before we get these poor flowers in the ground."

Setting a bucket of digging tools beside the rusty plow, Susan watched the youngster ease his wheelchair down the porch ramp. Danny looked nervous, a little pale. Both to be expected since the boy had barely been out of the house since his surgery.

Susan knew better than to ask if he needed help. Bodine men, she'd discovered, were stubborn, stoic, impossibly independent. The need for assistance was interpreted as an unacceptable weakness. Such machismo was hardly unique, particularly for the rugged individualists who had put their brand on this harsh, unforgiving land.

Nearly a week had passed since the drenching storm, and the ground had dried enough to make a sturdy foundation for Danny's wheelchair. Still, it was bumpy, uneven, not nearly as stable as the hardwood floors in the house.

Pretending not to notice the child's awkward navigation across the inhospitable terrain, Susan strolled to her car and retrieved several flats of colorful annuals. She'd worked some bags of soil amendments into the garden area earlier that morning. Now it was time for the fun part. "Marigolds, petunias, a climbing clematis vine…" she shifted the flats in her arms, hip-checked the car door shut, "…and a couple of blood-red geraniums. Did I forget anything?"

Danny grunted, pushed the wheels forward, then leaned against the chair's leather backrest, breathing heavily. He plucked a neatly folded sheet from his pocket, smoothed it open on his lap. "Umm, did you get the spiky purple things?"

"Stocks? Yes, I think so." Frowning, she scrutinized the crowded crush of tiny plants pressed into a cardboard box barely large enough to hold them. "Ah, yes, two six-packs of purple stocks. They haven't started to bloom yet, but by summer they should be incredibly beautiful."

She set the box of plants beside the plow, went back to her car to retrieve a worn blanket from the trunk.

"What's that for?" Danny asked as she spread it on the ground.

"It'll keep your cast from getting dirty while you help me plant these." Susan straightened, wiped a strand of hair from her moist cheek. "You didn't think I was going to do this all by myself, did you?"

A flicker of doubt crossed his gaze. "Umm, I dunno. I just figured I'd like, you know, tell you where to put stuff."

"You have a nifty throne, sire, but you're not king yet." She bent to flip up the left foot rest, and lower the right leg lift that held his cast out in a horizontal position. Danny flung an arm around her shoulders, balancing himself on his good leg as she lifted him from the chair. "Upsy daisy...wait, let me push the chair back...okay, I've got you, bucko. You're completely in my power."

She feigned an evil cackle that made him giggle, but only for a split second. He tightened his grip, nearly choking her. "Don't let me fall..."

"I won't, sweetie. I promise." She turned him

gently, using her free hand to brace his injured leg so it wouldn't be jarred as he awkwardly lowered himself onto the blanket. "Good job! I'm proud of you." She puffed out a breath, sat next to him. "First, let's fold part of the blanket over your cast to keep the dirt off...there, that's perfect. Now we're ready to garden. We should probably plant the flowering vine first, don't you think? That way it'll have plenty of room to wind up around this magnificent old plow, and we can arrange the annuals around the base of it, just like they are in your drawing."

"Okay." Danny watched Susan stand and retrieve a long-handled garden spade from an untidy tangle of implements strewn beside the barn. She'd just sunk the shovel blade into the earth when the child suddenly asked, "Do you think my mom is watching from heaven?"

Susan's foot slipped off the spade shoulder. She stumbled, righted herself, then leaned against the handle and regarded the child cautiously. "I believe that she is."

"Do you think she'll like what we're doing for her?"

"I never met your mother, Danny, but yes, I think she'll be very pleased indeed."

He considered that. "Okay. I just wondered, 'cause Dad never likes to talk about her much."

Dangerous ground here, Susan thought. She moistened her lips, bought a moment of time by scooping up a spadeful of dirt to pile beside the newly formed hole.

"I think," she said finally, "that it must be difficult for your father to talk about the loss of someone he loved."

"How come?"

"I would imagine he is very sad and that he misses her very much."

"I miss her, too." Danny reached for a six-pack of blooming marigolds, delicately traced the ruffled petals with his fingertip. "Sometimes when I ask Dad about her, he gets a funny look on his face and says we'll talk about it later. Only we never do."

Cupping both her palms over the tip of the spade handle, Susan rested her chin on the back of her hands. She wanted to comfort the child, but feared saying the wrong thing. She knew very little about Danny's mother beyond the photographs on the mantel, the faded decor in a house once vibrant with wild colors, and the remnants of a garden she had obviously loved.

A brief history included in school transcripts indicated that Danny had been around four when she died but had included no details. Several of Susan's colleagues and acquaintances had known Gail Bodine, but it had seemed inappropriate to question them about a woman who was supposedly nothing more than the deceased mother of one of Susan's pupils.

Without understanding the intricate dynamics of the family, or the circumstance of the woman's death, she had to choose her words very carefully or risk doing more harm than good, even though her heart went out to this lonely, confused little boy, and to his stoic, grieving father as well.

Gail Bodine had clearly been a very special woman to have been so deeply loved, so desperately needed by her family. On some level, Susan envied that, since she had never allowed herself to be needed. Or loved, for that matter. Eschewing emotional entanglements seemed a rational way to avoid disappointing people.

Susan had learned early in childhood that simply loving a person didn't mean that person would love you back. Sometimes you just weren't good enough or smart enough or pretty enough to keep from disappointing those you wanted most to please.

And when you weren't good enough or smart enough or pretty enough, people had a tendency to simply walk away.

She'd never known her own father. He'd left the family when she'd been an infant. Her stepfather had been her only male role model, a quiet, brooding man whose approval Susan had desperately—and fruitlessly—coveted. She'd been five when she'd come home from school to find her stepfather's closet empty and her mother in tears. It had been a turning point in her young life, an emotional betrayal that had shattered something vital deep inside.

Danny was also shattered, feeling betrayed. To a confused and frightened child, death was just another kind of abandonment. The emotions were all the same, a muddled tangle of grief, disillusionment, fear, anger. Guilt.

Always the guilt.

"Marigolds smell funny."

Susan blinked, glanced down at the pale youngster whose small body was dwarfed by the massive leg cast. "Smell funny?"

"Yeah. I think my mom liked them because they're yellow. Yellow was her favorite color."

Which explained the blinding cheeriness of the jonquil paint job in the guest room. "In that case, we'd better hurry up and get these flowers in the ground before they fade."

Danny smiled.

* * *

It had been a morning for frustration. An unusual warm snap early in the season had heralded a swarm of blood-sucking cowflies weeks before the annual shipment of insecticidal spray would be available. The vaccination process had come to a screeching halt when an angry heifer had literally crashed the squeeze chute to reach her bellowing baby. Now Jarod had to reweld several segments of the apparatus. Then Samuel had gotten into a fistfight with some young smart aleck who actually thought he could insult the wiry old codger's parentage without losing teeth in the process.

So Jarod had fired the smart aleck, assigned another of his men to drive the bloodied kid to the hospital some sixty miles away, and also lost the use of Samuel, who stubbornly refused treatment for a hand he pretended was only bruised, but that Jarod suspected was either broken or badly strained.

There was a word to describe mornings like this, a word he couldn't use in front of his son.

He jerked the steering wheel, bounced his truck around a sharp bend in the rutted road, and turned onto the scraped driveway climbing one of the few ridges rising about the flat rangeland. He cruised past the stand of poplars his granddaddy had planted, and pulled up beside the barn, noticing that Susan's battered old sedan was parked nearby.

He glanced at his watch, saw it was past three and wondered why she hadn't left at two, which was her usual schedule. His pulse beat a little faster just knowing she was here. It annoyed him, this physical manifestation her presence wrought without his permission. His fascination with her annoyed him.

Clearly, however, the fascination was returned. Jarod was a pragmatist, but he wasn't a fool. It wasn't a coincidence that Susan Mitchell had reinserted herself into his life. She had sought him out deliberately, and Jarod knew why.

Despite her denials, he firmly believed that Susan Mitchell wanted more of what they'd already shared in that dusky motel room.

The truth was that Jarod wanted that, too. Some nights the sensual memories made him break out in a cold sweat, the power of physical response to his desire was positively painful. What they'd shared had been terrific, wild and wonderfully passionate, yet exquisitely sweet and tender, everything a man could envision in a night to remember.

Yes, the sex had been great. But there had been something else to that experience, something that haunted him. Something that frightened him.

More than his body had been touched that night. Susan Mitchell had strummed a quiet chord deep in his soul. For the first time in more years than he could remember, Jarod had felt whole. Scary stuff for a man who'd vowed to keep his heart on a shelf for the rest of his natural life.

So Jarod charitably convinced himself that he understood why Susan would seek him out for more of something that had clearly been a magnificent experience, and solemnly vowed that when she finally made her intentions known, he would rebuff her as gently as possible.

All these thoughts meandered through his mind as he exited the truck and dragged awkward five-foot by four-foot tubular steel chute segments from the pickup bed.

Danny's voice startled him. "Dad's home!"

Jarod pivoted, automatically gazing from his shaded area beside the barn to the house. The porch was empty.

"Dad, Dad, come here! Look what we did!"

Stunned, Jarod realized that his son's voice was coming from in front of the barn. Except for the occasional foray onto the porch and trips for follow-up medical care, Danny hadn't been out of the house since the accident. Jarod had tried to coax him into a cruise around the ranch, or even a short walk up to the stables, but the boy had always gotten a horrified look on his face and refused.

"Dad, hurry! It's like, so awesome. You gotta see!"

Jarod wiped his hands on his jeans and strode forward. When he rounded the corner of the barn, he jerked to a stop, nearly gasped out loud in disbelief.

There was his son, seated on a dirt-covered blanket, surrounded by empty fertilizer bags and waving a small garden shovel as if it were the holy grail. Jarod was so stunned by the sight he barely noticed the splash of color toward which the boy was gesturing wildly.

He did, however, notice the woman standing nearby, twisting her fingers together. Her face was pale, her gaze was cautious. She said nothing.

"Look, Dad, it's just like it used to be! Marigolds and pansies and petunias and those funny little white things..." He frowned, angled a questioning look at Susan.

"Baby's breath." Her reply was so soft Jarod barely heard.

"Yeah, baby's breath." Danny was pink with excitement. "Momma is happy now, isn't she? I mean, if she's looking down from heaven, she's gotta be real happy, 'cause all her favorite flowers are planted just the way she likes them.''

A chill of realization slipped down his spine. He finally focused on the object of his son's attention and felt the breath hiss out of his lungs. He closed his eyes for a moment, rubbed them with the heels of his hands, then looked again, and was swept into a vortex of memories.

Gail had loved flowers. As soon as the snow melted, pots of hardy perennials appeared on the front porch. When the ground thawed, a riot of color would ribbon around the rusty old plow, purple and yellow, orange and red, splashes of beauty and wonder that Gail had nurtured throughout the growing season.

Flowers made her feel alive, she had said, a touch of beauty in a land that was otherwise devoid of it.

Her garden had been an escape from a life too lonely, too brutal to be faced on its own terms. Jarod had resented the beauty Gail created around them, because it had been a cruel reminder that the woman he loved more than life itself and the land that was as much a part of him as his own blood did not belong together.

''Dad?''

Jarod blinked, realized that Danny's grin of delight had faded into a worried frown.

''Don't you like it, Dad?''

''I, ah, I'm just surprised, that's all.''

''It's just like Momma used to do it. Look, I drew it all out.'' Danny whipped a folded paper out of his shirt pocket, held it out with a hopeful look in his eyes. ''Maybe I didn't remember right...?''

A lump formed in his throat as he opened the paper

and saw the crayoned picture his son had drawn. It was perfect, an accurate portrayal of the colors and textures Gail had used in the same area so many years ago. The child had even shown the climbing vine that wound around the plow which was the centerpiece of the flowered plot.

Danny had been so very young, barely four years old. It hadn't occurred to Jarod that he'd recall such vivid details. He licked his lips, swallowed hard. He looked directly at Susan.

She caught the accusation in his gaze and answered it quietly, with only a slight slump of her shoulders. "I realize I should have asked your permission before encouraging Danny's project, but I didn't want to spoil the surprise. He thought it would please you."

"It does please me," Jarod said. The words nearly choked him, but it wasn't really a lie. For the first time in weeks his son had actually confronted his fear and ventured out of the house. Even more important was the light of excitement in his eyes, excitement that Jarod hadn't seen since before the accident.

He didn't know what magic Susan Mitchell had cast to accomplish this monumental feat, and frankly he didn't care. All that mattered was that his son had turned a corner in his recovery.

In his heart, Jarod knew he had Susan to thank for that. "The garden is beautiful, son. It's perfect, exactly as your mother would have done it."

The relief in Danny's eyes nearly broke Jarod's heart. "So Momma will be happy, right?"

Jarod caught the anxiety in Susan's eyes. Her look begged him to assure the child that his mother would indeed be happy even if it wasn't true. "Your mother would be very proud of you, just as I am."

Danny beamed.

From the corner of his eye Jarod saw Susan turn away. She sniffed, wiped her face with the back of her hand. She began to gather up the empty bags and gardening implements.

"I think it's time for a certain young man to take a well-earned break," she said with a cheeriness that seemed a trifle overdone. Tucking squashed plastic bags under her arm, she propped the garden spade against the barn wall. A quick glimpse at her face confirmed that her eyes were red.

"I'm getting a little hungry," Danny said. "I think we kinda forgot to eat lunch."

"I think you're right." Susan discreetly touched the corner of her eye, as if merely flicking away a buzzing insect. "Last time I looked, Martha was rolling out a pie crust, and there was a bowl of apples on the table. It seems to me that a slab of warm pie and a glass of cold milk would make a nice reward for a job well done."

"Sounds like a winner." Jarod strode forward, lifted his son into the wheelchair, only to have Danny wave him off when he started to push his son's chair toward the ramp.

"I can do it," the boy insisted.

"Of course you can." Jarod stepped back, flexed his fingers at his side, watched the youngster weave his way up the porch ramp, struggle with the screen door for a few moments before disappearing into the house.

He heard a sigh of relief and realized it had come from himself. It was incredibly difficult knowing when to step forward, when to step back. Children had to evolve toward independence. Jarod knew that. But it was so damned hard to let go, or to watch one's child struggle with the challenge of simply growing up.

Behind him, Susan whispered quietly, words meant to travel only to Jarod's ears and not beyond. "That was probably one of the most generous, selfless and loving acts I've ever seen in my life."

He glanced over his shoulder, saw the sheen of moisture in her eyes. A tear slipped onto her cheek. This time she didn't bother to wipe it away.

Jarod spoke cautiously. "I don't understand what you mean."

A shuddering breath shook her fragile body. She rubbed her upper arms, as if she was suddenly chilled. "I saw your face when you first realized what Danny had done. The pain in your eyes cut like a knife. You were shattered."

As true as that was, Jarod felt compelled to argue the point. "I was merely surprised, that's all. It hadn't occurred to me that Danny had been old enough to remember the details of things like what color of flowers his mother planted, and where she planted them."

"It was more than that. For a split second in time, you weren't even here. You were somewhere else, reliving something exquisitely painful." She took a breath, folded her arms, tore her gaze away from him to stare out toward the stables, nearly a quarter of a mile away. "I'm so terribly sorry. I should have realized that Danny's surprise could dredge up memories of all that you had lost."

Perceptive she was, Jarod thought, able to look into a man's soul and read all that he kept private from the world. That fascinated him. It also scared the hell out of him. "I said I was just surprised. Anything else you think you saw is nothing more than a vivid imagination run amuck.''

She smiled, but continued to gaze out toward the horizon. "You pushed your own feelings aside and gave your son exactly what he needed. You made him feel special, important, loved."

"Danny *is* special. He *is* important and he *is* loved."

"Yes," she murmured. "I know that." She tilted her head just enough to stare deeply into his eyes. "You really are one of those rare men who actually deserve the title of parent."

The unexpected comment startled him. He blinked, opened his mouth, then closed it when the only sound to emerge was a peculiar gurgle. He touched his thumb to the brim of his hat, an absentminded gesture that he was barely aware of.

"Well," he said finally. "I guess that was a compliment. If so, I thank you. If not, don't bother to edify me. I'd rather stick with the delusion that there's something about me you like beyond the obvious."

Her eyes widened. "The obvious?"

Oh, hell. He couldn't suppress a snort of annoyance at himself. "That kind of slipped out. Sorry. I know we agreed not to talk about...well...things that we agreed not to talk about."

"And those things would be...?"

"You know."

"Yes, I think I do know, but I'd like to hear you say it out loud anyway." She was pale, swaying slightly, still twisting her hands together.

Jarod glanced over his shoulder, saw the front door to the house was safely closed. "Look, I understand that we shared something very pleasant, and that it's normal to want to continue that. But I'm not ready for a relationship right now. I know that's disappointing to you— What's so damned funny?''

She covered her grin, turned away and let loose a chuckle that raised every hackle on Jarod's nape.

When she straightened, she wiped her forehead, and was still smiling as she shook her head. ''The male ego never ceases to amaze me. You actually believe I tracked you down because you were so virile, so irresistibly sexy that despite my repeated protests to the contrary I simply could not live without the sensual seduction of your masculine magnificence?''

Jarod did not like the direction this conversation had taken. ''Well I sure as hell don't believe you showed up on my doorstep out of happenstance *just* to tutor my son.''

Her smile faded, along with all traces of color from cheeks that were now the pallid hue of eggshells. ''You're right, I didn't.''

''Aha.'' Satisfied, he bobbed his head, tugged his hat down. ''I knew it.''

''I'm here because I wanted to know what kind of a man you really were, Jarod Bodine, and what kind of a father you were to your son.''

Taken aback, he felt his jaw slacken. ''Why in hell is that your business?''

''It's my business,'' she said quietly. She wobbled, swayed, touched her pale forehead with the back of her hand. ''Because I'm carrying your child.''

With that stunning pronouncement, Susan's eyes rolled back in her head, and she fainted.

Chapter Five

The moan awakened her. Icy moisture touched her face.

Susan turned away from the annoyance, tried to bury her head in the pillow. Evasive maneuvers had no effect. The clammy coldness continued to swab her forehead, her cheek, the corners of her dry mouth. She feebly swatted it away, forced herself to squint into a room where blinding sunlight bounced off vivid yellow walls.

She heard the moan again and realized it had come from her.

Disoriented, she struggled into a sitting position, shading eyes that couldn't quite focus on the broadshouldered silhouette looming over her.

The silhouette spoke. "Feeling better?"

Alerted by the familiar voice, she tensed. "Jarod?"

"None other." The response was issued in a flat monotone.

As Susan's eyes became accustomed to the brightness, she realized that she was at the Bodine ranch in the guest room where she'd spent a restless night during last week's storm. "What happened?"

"You fainted." He set a wadded washcloth on the nightstand, regarded her for a moment. "Not surprising under the circumstances."

"What circumstances?" The moment she blurted the words her memory flooded back.

Because I'm carrying your child.

Groaning, she flopped back onto the pillows, flung her arm across her eyes. Why on earth had she told him? She hadn't meant to, not yet, not until she was certain that Jarod was the kind of man worthy of inclusion into her child's life.

Except the child wasn't simply hers; it was Jarod's child, too.

Susan moistened her lips, kept her eyes covered as she spoke. "I'm sorry. I hadn't planned to disclose that tidbit of information in such a blunt manner."

Boots shuffled across the hardwood floor. She heard the sound of water being poured into a glass. "I see." More booted footsteps. "Here, drink this."

She peeked out from under her forearm, saw the water glass in his hand. As much as she'd have liked to refuse the offer to avoid sitting up and actually looking at him, her throat was utterly parched.

Pushing herself upright, she accepted the glass while avoiding his gaze, and drank until she'd drained the final drop. After she'd set the empty glass on the nightstand, she wiped her mouth with the back of a shaky hand. "Thank you."

"Would you like more?"

She shook her head, noticed that her fingernails were filthy. Gardening played hell with a manicure. She should have used gloves.

"Well?"

"Well what?" She'd have to soak her fingertips in detergent to get rid of the dirt stains.

Jarod stepped sideways, blocking the late-afternoon sun rays streaming through the window. His shadow fell across Susan like a cold, dark shroud. "You've just tossed an explosive bomb into my life. I'd like to discuss it."

"What would you like to know?"

"For starters, I'd like to know why you think the child is mine."

A furious heat crawled up her throat, blossomed along her jawbone. It was a question he had every right to ask. She wondered why she hadn't expected it. "I *think* that the child is yours because the child *is* yours."

For a moment the silence was deafening. When Jarod finally spoke, his voice was soft, level, frighteningly calm. "You expect me to simply take your word for that?"

The trembling in her hands slipped up to her shoulders, then back down her spine until her entire body vibrated. "I don't expect anything, actually. For reasons that I'm now beginning to question, I decided that you deserved to know that you had fathered a child."

Jarod wiped his face with his palms, then peered over his fingertips. "Gail and I spent three years trying to conceive Danny. Now you waltz into my life after we spent one night together...you'll forgive me if I find this situation difficult to accept." He moistened his lips, shook his head. "It isn't possible. We used precautions."

"Contraceptives aren't foolproof." God, she was tired. And she was becoming nauseous again. She hated that. "Look, maybe the condom slipped, maybe some smart aleck poked a pin through the box while it was still on the drugstore shelf. I don't know, and at this point I don't care. It happened. Accept it or not, it makes no difference to me." She sat up, swung her feet onto the floor and gripped the mattress as the room gyrated around her.

Jarod could move fast for a big man. In the space of a heartbeat he'd crossed the room and taken hold of her shoulders. "Lie back." It was murmured softly, with obvious concern.

"Can't." Susan pressed one hand to her belly, the other covered her mouth. "I'm sick."

Before her final word was spoken, Jarod had slipped an arm around her waist and lifted her to her feet. He half carried her down the hall, cradled her in his arms while she was violently ill.

Afterward, Susan sagged against the sink, weak and trembling.

She heard Danny's high-pitched voice and realized the child's wheelchair was blocking the open doorway. "What's wrong with Miss Mitchell? Does she got the flu or something?"

"She's not feeling well, son."

"She's gonna be okay, isn't she? I mean, she's not gonna die or anything?" A touch of panic edged the child's voice.

"Miss Mitchell will be just fine, Danny. Let's go see if Martha needs any help in the kitchen."

A glance in the mirror confirmed that Jarod was ushering the child away. Susan could have wept in relief when he closed the door behind him, giving her some much-needed privacy.

Better late than never, she supposed.

Groaning, she folded her arms over the cool sink and bent to rest her forehead on one elbow. Jarod had actually held her, murmured words of comfort the way a gentle parent would do for a sick little child. If humiliation had been fatal, she'd have expired on the spot.

Well, there was nothing to be done about it now.

After allowing herself a few minutes to wash her face, rinse her mouth, and smooth back her gritty hair, she felt slightly more human as she emerged to face the chaos her unplanned announcement had wrought.

She heard voices from the kitchen, Danny's high-pitched concern about her condition offset by Jarod's quiet reassurance and Martha's normal grumbling about dirt tracks on her clean floor.

Susan paused in the hallway just outside the kitchen door. She took several calming breaths, pasted a pleasant expression on her face and entered. All conversation instantly ceased. Three sets of eyes were focused on her: worried, mildly curious, cynically suspicious.

She edged toward the kitchen table on which her notebooks and assignment folders were stacked. "Words cannot express how sorry I am to have created such a disruption, so I'll just gather my things—"

Danny pivoted his chair around. "Are you better now? I mean, you looked all white and stuff when Dad carried you in. I thought you were a goner for sure."

The image of being carried in Jarod's arms was oddly appealing. On some level Susan was sorry to have been unconscious during an experience that under different circumstances might have been quite pleasant.

Stunned by the inappropriate thoughts, she felt her skin heat, tried to focus her attention on the wide-eyed child who was studying her with obvious anxiety. "I'm really fine, Danny. I skipped lunch today, and I guess I overdid our gardening adventure, that's all."

The harsh scrape of a chair startled her. Jarod pushed away from the table. He stood, regarding her with an expression that could have been impassive, angry or both. "Skipping meals is unacceptable. You need proper nourishment."

Even Martha appeared startled by the pronouncement—and had every right to be considering the harried housekeeper frequently complained that Jarod was too busy to enjoy the fine meals she prepared for him. Martha stared at the scowling man, flicked a bewildered glance at Susan, then she closed her gaping mouth and scoured the kitchen sink in silence.

Danny's surprise was neither constrained nor silent. "Wow, how come you're using your dad voice on Miss Mitchell? Are you mad at her or something?"

Jarod actually blushed. "No, of course not. I, er, was simply, ah, offering information."

Susan clasped her hands together, managed a tight smile. "And excellent information it is. Thank you for sharing that, Jarod. I'll certainly keep it in mind."

Jarod grunted, shoved the chair back under the table and strode toward the doorway leading into the hall. As he passed Susan, he paused, spoke without looking at her. "May I have a moment of your time? In my office, please."

"Your office?" She wasn't familiar with the room

in question, but that wasn't surprising. The Bodine home was old, but it was quite large. There was one entire wing of the house into which Susan had never ventured.

"It's through that funny door in the living room," Danny said helpfully. "Dad doesn't let hardly anybody go in there. He must really like you."

Susan felt sick again. She returned the boy's happy grin with a thin smile of her own, then followed a stiff-shouldered Jarod through the living area to the door Danny had described and into a large, cluttered room with a messy desk, a computer, a couple of lounge chairs, a sofa and a row of file cabinets.

Jarod went directly to the desk, shoved some papers from one side to the other and began to flip through a Rolodex beside what appeared to be a stack of ledgers.

Susan shuffled her feet, cleared her throat. "Is Danny allowed to use the computer? It might be very helpful for his schoolwork—"

"Danny has a computer in his bedroom."

"Oh. He never mentioned that, but I should have presumed as much."

"Presumed?" He spoke without favoring her with a glance, while scribbling on a scratchpad. "Why?"

"Well, computers are becoming an integral part of both business and classroom, at least for those who can afford them, which you certainly can."

His head snapped around. "What's that supposed to mean?"

"Excuse me?"

"You found it necessary to comment on what I could afford." He eyed her with suspicion, took a step forward. "Why is that?"

She stared at him, astonished and infuriated by the

implication. "Because my plan to blackmail you out of every red cent depends upon your financial ability to buy your son a stupid computer, of course. That's what us money-grubbing women of loose morals do when they finally get themselves pregnant, isn't it?"

Jarod's eyes widened, then narrowed. He ripped a sheet from the scratchpad, then stepped past her to close the office door. "You appear to be reading a great deal into a simple question."

"Hormones. We pregnant folks always overreact. If you weren't implying that my innocent comment reflected an unhealthy interest in your financial affairs, then I misunderstood and I apologize." She watched his guilty gaze skitter away. "Did I misunderstand your concern?"

"No."

"I didn't think so."

He drew in a breath, continued to avoid her gaze. "Do you have an obstetrician?"

"I don't believe that's any of your business, but I will charitably reply anyway. Yes, I do."

"Who is it?"

"Now that really is none of your business."

Now he looked at her, long and hard. Unidentifiable emotion flickered through his gaze, then disappeared behind an inscrutable veil. "Your health and the health of the child you carry are very much my business." He spoke firmly, then added, "If the child is mine."

Although Susan understood his skepticism, it continued to wound her nonetheless. "I guess you'll just have to take my word for it. Or not." She turned to grasp the doorknob. "It honestly doesn't matter to me one way or the other."

Crossing the room in two giant steps, he covered

her hand with his own, preventing her from opening the door. "It matters very much." He lifted her hand, pressed the scratch paper on which he'd been scribbling into her palm.

Susan studied the name and phone number that he'd written. "Who is Dr. Bingham?"

"He's our family practitioner. He'll make the arrangements for whatever tests each of us must have."

The gist of that comment slipped slowly into her mind. When she fully grasped its meaning, her palms turned icy. "Tests to confirm paternity."

"Yes."

It was a perfectly prudent request. Rationally, Susan understood that. Emotionally, it tore her up inside. She had no idea why. "I…understand."

Jarod shifted his stance, reached out to lift her chin with exquisite gentleness. When she continued to look past him into thin air, he urged her face around until she had little choice but to gaze into soft gray eyes that were surprisingly tender.

"No, I don't think you do understand," he said. "I'm not trying to hurt you or insult you. This child…our child…will become one of my heirs, just like Danny. Someday everything I own, everything my father and his father before him owned, will belong to my children. All of my children. There must never be any question of legitimacy. Not now, not ever."

Tears welled in Susan's eyes. She chalked it up to those damnable hormones, but the truth was that she was deeply touched. Some people might have seen Jarod's concern as self-serving, view him as hoping that the tests would exclude him from the gene pool rather than confirm his paternity.

But Susan saw something besides tenderness in his

eyes. She saw a glimmer of restrained joy. It touched her to the core.

"You want this child," she whispered. "You're afraid to get your hopes up until you see the test results, but deep down you really, truly want this child to be yours."

Jarod stepped back, displayed a sudden urge to adjust his battered headgear. "Children are a blessing," he said finally. "Any man would be proud to have as many as the Lord sees fit to give him."

"Not any man." Susan cringed at the edge in her voice, forced a softer tone. "You're a good person, Jarod Bodine, and a wonderful father. I'll do what you ask and schedule the test as soon as possible."

He opened his mouth as if to thank her, but all that came out was an emotional croak that seemed to aggravate him immensely. He frowned, yanked on his hat again, hooked his thumbs in the pockets of his dusty jeans. "Who else knows about this?"

"Knows about what, my pregnancy or your participation in it?"

"Both."

"My obstetrician knows I'm pregnant, of course. I haven't shared any further information with her. Nobody else knows." She paused as he offered a brusque nod. "Except my sister."

His torso straightened. "Your sister?"

"Yes, but don't worry. My sister Laura isn't a gossip. Besides, she lives in New York."

"A New Yorker?" He looked horrified.

"She lives upstate, almost as rural in some spots as Montana." She teased him with a smile. "Don't worry, your child won't grow up dodging Times Square traffic and roller blading in Central Park."

For a moment he stared at her as if she'd sprouted antlers. "You're moving to New York?"

Susan immediately realized that she'd said the wrong thing at the wrong time. Again. Good timing was clearly not her forte. "My sister and her husband have invited me to stay with them until the baby is born and I'm back on my feet financially."

His shattered expression surprised her. "I don't understand. I thought you liked Montana. I thought you were happy here."

"I am happy here. That's not the point."

"It's the only point that matters."

"I wish it was that easy."

She smiled, more to keep from crying than to display wry amusement. There was nothing humorous in a situation that on the one hand offered her child a relationship with a magnificent father, then limited that relationship by putting a thousand miles between them.

"I really don't have a lot of options here, Jarod. There isn't much call for pregnant, unmarried teachers around here, or anywhere else for that matter. As soon as my condition becomes obvious, I'll be out of a job. Montana is a big state, but in many ways it's also like a small town. Even after the baby is born it will be difficult for me to get another teaching position. There's no way I'll even be able to support myself here, let alone support a child."

He studied her with eyes annoyingly veiled, unreadable. "No child of mine will ever go hungry. I suspect you know that much about me."

She met his gaze without wavering. "And no child of mine will ever be forced to rely on the charity of an absent father to put food on the table. I suspect you know that much about me.''

He considered that. ''Actually, neither of us knows a damned thing about the other, do we?''

Oddly deflated, Susan focused her attention on details of the office. Old photographs on the wall, pictures of men and of horses, a grainy snapshot of a particularly homely bull, a broad-shouldered older man with a craggy face and a solemn expression much like the one Jarod now wore. ''I know that you love your son, that there is nothing you wouldn't do to keep him safe and happy. Beyond that, you're right. We don't know much about each other.''

''A pretty shaky foundation on which to start a family, isn't it?''

The impact of his comment sank in slowly. She swung her gaze around, meeting his startled gaze. ''Start a family?''

Having been caught studying her, he quickly looked away. ''We'll discuss this later. You should rest now. I'll have one of the men drive you home.''

''Thank you for your concern, but I'm quite capable of deciding when I require rest and of driving myself home.''

''You'll either allow someone to escort you, or you can rest in the guest room until your skin has some color beyond that of wet chalk and your eyes can focus without crossing.''

''You have no right to issue orders to me.''

''That's true, but you are not well enough to traverse forty miles of unpleasant road alone at the moment, and under normal circumstances I suspect you'd be the first to admit it.''

She couldn't dispute his assessment. Her knees were

trembling, her skin was clammy, and she felt wobbly enough to fall over in a mild breeze.

Still, his arrogance irked her. The fact that he was right played only a secondary role in her annoyance.

Jarod also looked annoyed. Beneath the brim of his hat, his forehead creased into a frown, his lips were stretched tight, his jawline taut as fresh-pulled fence wire. Angry or not, he was just about the most appealing man Susan had ever laid eyes on. And the most frustrating.

Without warning Jarod yanked off his hat, slapped his thigh with it, then flung it onto the desk. He muttered an oath, bent over his desk with both hands flat on the surface.

After a moment, he took a deep breath, straightened and faced her. "I'm not handling this very well, am I?"

The question startled her. "I...I don't know how something like this should be handled."

He nodded. "I'm not the most tactful person. I consider myself to be brusque on occasion, although Martha says I tend to be downright rude. I don't mean to be. If I've hurt you, I'm sorry."

The abrupt change in his demeanor threw Susan another emotional curve. She had no idea how to respond, so said nothing.

"Life doesn't always go the way we've planned," Jarod said. "We'll have to make the best of this."

Unnerved by the resigned expression on his face, the deceptive calm of his voice, Susan remained silent.

"I don't want this to be more difficult than it has to be. Once the test results are confirmed, I'll make the arrangements as discreetly as possible."

A chill slipped down her spine. "Arrangements?"

Jarod favored her with a glance. "I thought you understood. Bodines have held a position of esteem in this county for generations. Ours is a respected family, a respected name. I'll not allow it to be tainted or dishonored, nor will any child of mine suffer the stigma of illegitimacy."

Susan laid a protective hand over her belly. "What…what are you saying?"

"I thought I'd made myself quite clear."

"I'm a little slow today," she whispered. "What exactly are you talking about?"

He seemed taken aback. "Why, our marriage, of course."

"Marriage?" The room swam, Susan stumbled backward against a wooden chair, sat down hard. "You are actually suggesting that we get married?"

"I'm afraid you've misunderstood me again," he said quietly. "If the child is mine, you and I will be married as quickly as the law allows. This is not a suggestion. It is a fact."

Chapter Six

Sunlight glinted from the rear window of the pickup truck following Susan's sedan down the rutted ranch road. Jarod watched from the porch until both vehicles had disappeared from view.

He felt as if he'd swallowed a brick. Guilt was not a unique sensation to a man burdened with responsibility since the day he'd been born. So many responsibilities to so many people who depended upon him. Some he had created for himself. Some he had inherited, like his duty to nourish the land, to continue what his father and grandfather had begun.

The ranch had been the focus of their lives, yet the success that had come so easily for them continued to elude Jarod. Costs were up; prices were down. Winters had been too harsh; summers too dry. The land itself was withering under his stewardship. His performance as a son and heir, as a Bodine, had been lackluster, to say the least.

He'd also failed in his family obligations, failed miserably and in so many ways. Because he had failed as a husband, a son was motherless; because he'd failed as a father, a child desperate for attention had nearly been killed.

And because he'd failed as a man, a woman's life had been ruined.

Why was it, Jarod wondered, that he had this innate talent for destroying everything and everybody that he loved most?

Not that he loved Susan Mitchell. Romantic love was not an emotion Jarod was willing to allow into his life, into his heart, ever again.

Still, he cared about her. There was something haunting about Susan, something stirring about the way she'd snap a wry retort to set him back on his heels, or angle an appreciative glance when he'd finally said something witty instead of just plain stupid. A smile, a laugh, a quiet blush gave his boots wings for the rest of the day.

What attracted him most to Susan wasn't her breathtaking smile or exotic eyes so bright a man could lose his soul in them. It was the way she instinctively understood the heart of a lonely, isolated youngster and had gently guided him out of his self-imposed shell of fear.

Jarod descended the porch steps, found himself standing in front of the freshly turned earth bristling with new color, a riot of blooming yellows, rusty orange, scarlet and crimson. Happy colors, vibrant colors.

Colors that broke Jarod's heart.

Danny's crayoned drawing was proudly displayed in the kitchen, a collage of childlike squiggles and shaky circles that reflected the reality of that long-ago garden so accurately that it gave Jarod goose bumps. Susan had warned Jarod that Danny recalled more of his mother's life, and of her death, than Jarod wanted to believe.

Susan had clearly been right.

Jarod didn't hear Martha's approach until she spoke. "The pot roast is simmering," she muttered from a spot a few feet behind him. "Throw a few pared potatoes and carrots in about an hour before supper time. 'Tis a drill you know by now."

"Thanks." He inhaled deeply, pretended to be gazing at the stable several hundred yards north of the house. A couple of ranch hands were unloading oat bags from a fork lift. "Is Danny doing his homework?"

"If Miss Mitchell assigned the study of action comic books, then aye, that he is." She glanced down the road. "I'll be going now. 'Tis time to start Samuel's supper, although I suspect he won't be home to taste it before it grows cold."

"I'm sorry about sending him to town so late in the day. He'll get overtime pay, though."

"And well he should." She issued a snort, feigning an indignance Jarod knew she didn't feel. "'Tis difficult enough setting a meal schedule for cowboys."

"Ranching engineers, if you please." Jarod slipped a chummy arm around the woman's stocky shoulders. "We Bodines are a pretentious lot."

"Aye, that's the truth." She laughed, dusted her hands on her slacks. "Miss Mitchell is pregnant, isn't she?"

Jarod removed his arm from Martha's shoulders, hoping to disguise the involuntary tightening of his muscles. He feigned great interest in the oat-unloading exercise, although he held no illusion that Martha would be fooled by the pretense. "The stable roof is sagging over the tack barn again. Remind me to have Samuel check for cracked rafters. The snow was heavy this winter."

"Changing the topic, are we? Typical, it is." Martha sighed, knocked her boot against a rock to dislodge a dirt clod. "Ignore the question if you've a mind to, makes no difference to me. I raised four wee ones of my own, so pregnancy is no mystery to me. Everyone in the county will be knowing soon enough, and that's a fact." Martha sniffed the air, pursed her lips. "You'd be the proud papa, I'm guessing."

Jarod clamped his teeth together, said nothing.

Martha nodded. "Aye, that much was clear when you sent Samuel to see her home instead of going yourself. Men need some quiet think-time when they learn a new wee one is on the way."

Jarod had no choice but to relent. When Martha got her teeth into a topic, she'd shake the damned thing dead. "I asked Samuel to escort her home because I presumed Susan would be more comfortable with him than with me."

"And why would she be unhappy with such a sweet soul as yourself, hmm?"

He slipped her a wry smile. "Under the circumstances, can you blame her?"

Martha shrugged. "Unless things have changed since my youth, breeding babies requires a partnership. Besides, Miss Mitchell doesn't strike me as the type to blame others without shouldering her own share."

That much was true, although a niggling anger secretly seeped through Jarod. For nearly a month Susan had been tutoring Danny, or at least going through the motions of tutoring him, and all the while she'd been covertly sizing up Jarod's life, his ability as a father, his worth as a human being. He resented that, resented it deeply. "I suppose I should be thankful she told me in the first place."

"And who else would she be telling? You're the daddy."

"Apparently biological factors don't automatically confer the rights of fatherhood, at least not in Susan's mind. She actually had the audacity to audition me, size up my parental potential, as it were."

The bitter edge on his voice clearly startled Martha. From the corner of his eye Jarod saw her head twist sharply, and felt her disapproving frown rake the side of his face.

"Would you be having facts to support such a pompous presumption?"

Jarod thumbed his hat back a notch. "Susan told me that if I hadn't passed her damned test, she'd have slipped out of my life forever, and taken my child with her." He folded his arms, clenched his jaw. "Is that fact enough for you?"

Beside him, Martha yanked a crumpled handkerchief from her shirt pocket, mopped her face with it. "Ah, so that's what irks you, is it? She didn't go blurting the news at the sight of your studly face. Or perhaps you're not believing any woman seduced by such irresistible machismo could consider a life without it?"

Jarod glared at her. "I have a right to a relationship with my own child."

"'Tis true enough." Martha returned the wadded handkerchief to her pocket. "It seems Miss Mitchell came to the same conclusion, so what would you be huffing about?"

"I do not huff."

"All men huff. 'Tis their nature."

Jarod glumly shoved his hands in his pockets. "The child may not even be mine."

"You know that it is."

Jarod tipped his hat back, squinted into the late-afternoon sun. Memories flooded back, memories of soft sighs, soul-shaking groans, memories of kisses so sweet he could still taste them, of seeking hands, soft fingers, caresses so exquisite that his skin tingled at the thought. The world had exploded that night, morphed into a dimension beyond anything he'd ever experienced.

They had created an emotional connection that night; and they had created a life.

Perhaps Jarod shouldn't be happy about that, but he was. It was the happiness that terrified him.

Exhaustion set in easily nowadays. Susan mildly resented that. She didn't like the feeling of being powerless, of having to acquiesce to the dictates of a body that had always been adequate to her needs.

She studied a can of chili, then recalled that she'd suffered two unpleasant bouts of heartburn already this week. She returned the chili to the shelf and was just about to prepare a boring but benign grilled cheese sandwich when the doorbell rang.

It was only a few steps from the small corner kitchen across the living area of her meager apartment. She yanked the door open, expecting to see her packrat neighbor who inevitably appeared to borrow whatever ingredients were required to prepare her family's evening meal. "Whatever you need, hon, I'm fresh out. I haven't been to the market in days…"

Her protest dissipated into stunned silence.

Jarod shifted a bouquet of tissue-wrapped flowers from one hand to the other, cleared his throat, and stretched his lips into the semblance of a smile. "Hi."

Since Susan hadn't even seen so much as Jarod's shadow in the two weeks since he'd learned about her pregnancy, it took a moment to find her voice. "What are you doing here?"

"I'm courting you." He thrust out the flowers like an afterthought and with less elegance than one would use in offering an alfalfa chip to a hungry steer. "I have dinner reservations at the Steak House."

Susan did not reach for the flowers. "How nice for you. Have a good time."

Jarod frowned. "Let me rephrase that. *We* have dinner reservations at the Steak House. Didn't you get my message?"

"Message?" She glanced at the blinking red light on her telephone answering machine. "Ah, well, actually no. I just got home from a PTA meeting."

"You shouldn't work such long hours. It's not good for you." To Susan's shock, Jarod brushed past her, strode into the apartment. "Since we are making our public debut, you might want to change into something a little dressier. And running a comb through your hair wouldn't hurt."

Susan automatically brushed a mussed tendril from her face, tucked it behind her ear. She didn't know if she was more galled by his comments or by embarrassment that Jarod had caught her looking so unkempt. "It's been a long day. I wasn't expecting company."

"You would have if you'd check your messages once in a while." He walked into the kitchen as if he owned it, began opening her cupboard doors.

She would have commented on his chutzpah had she not been focused on something else he'd said. "What do you mean, our public debut?"

Jarod yanked out an ugly plastic pitcher, eyed it with disdain. "I guess this will have to do. You don't seem to have a big supply of flower vases."

"Don't put them in there. I don't want my orange juice tasting like gladiola stems." Frustrated, she brushed past him, retrieved an empty coffee can and plopped it on the counter.

Jarod stared at it. "How fashionable."

"*Chic* is my middle name. Now, are you going to answer my questions or should I play my message tape?"

He laid the bouquet beside the empty can, wrinkled his nose at a pile of dirty dishes in the sink. "The message merely pointed out that it would be helpful to public opinion if we're seen around town together once or twice before the wedding."

"Before the—?" She shook her head. "You really are the most arrogant man I've ever met."

"An arrogant man would presume that you wanted to marry him. I hold no such illusion." He filled the coffee can with water, tore off the tissue encumbering the stems and plopped the bouquet into the can without ceremony. "I won't subject our child to the legal quandary and stigma of illegitimacy. I thought I made myself clear on that matter."

"And I thought I made myself clear as well." Susan

pivoted to face him, planted her hands on what was left of her waist, uncomfortably aware of the increasingly noticeable swelling beneath her loose tunic. "I do not want to get married, Jarod. Not to you, not to anyone, not now, not ever. Marriage is an emotional abdication leading to inevitable disaster. I want nothing to do with it."

"For once we agree on something." He sighed, propped a noticeably lean and appealing hip against her counter. "I don't want to get married any more than you do. At this point what we want doesn't much count. What does count is what the child needs, what every child needs, the security of two nurturing parents who love her."

"I don't dispute that, but—" Susan swayed, blinked. "Her?"

Jarod glanced away, tugged at the bolo tie accenting his western-style shirt. "Nice photographs," he murmured, eyeing the three graduation pictures adorning the living-room wall. "Are those your sisters?"

"You referred to the baby as her. Why?"

"The one with long hair looks a lot like you. The other one, not so much. They're both lovely, though."

"Laura and I are full sisters. Catrina and I are half sisters."

"So you come from a broken home?"

"Not so much broken as totally shattered and the pieces stomped into dust. But out of chaos comes strength. You'd be surprised what a family of four determined females can do when they put their collective minds to it."

Jarod glanced at her, both surprise and respect mirrored in his gaze. "You must all be very close."

"We are."

"I've always wished I had siblings."

"You don't have any?"

He shook his head. "My parents had a child before me. A baby boy. His name was Chad Michael. He was stillborn."

"I'm sorry."

He shrugged, but a glaze of sorrow veiled his eyes. "I don't think my parents ever recovered from the loss. I wasn't conceived for another ten years. I never knew if that was by accident or design."

His pensive expression touched her. "Do you feel as if you were unwanted?"

"No, not at all. I was spoiled rotten, given everything a child could desire. My parents were older than those of my friends, but they were loving, supportive, wonderful. But I don't doubt that it must have been difficult on them raising a child when most people their age were enjoying grandchildren. My biggest disappointment is that they died before Danny was born. They would have doted on him."

Susan smiled. In truth, Danny was doted on quite enough. Between an adoring father whose attempts at discipline were half-hearted at best, and the constant attentions of Martha and Samuel, who'd taken over the pseudo-grandparent role with admirable enthusiasm, Danny had no shortage of love and adoration.

Unfortunately, love doesn't necessarily translate into understanding. Despite Jarod's undisputed love for his son, Susan suspected he didn't truly understand the boy, couldn't quite grasp the elusive fact that his offspring was not a clone of himself.

"Grandparents are a blessing," Susan said quietly.

"Yes. Danny never knew his."

Susan was sorry to hear that. It seemed a shame that

the son of a man for whom a family clearly meant so much had been deprived of knowing so many members of his own.

Still, he'd had two parents who cherished him. That was a blessing in itself. "The only grandparent we ever knew was my mom's mother, a wily old woman who raised six children and still worked in a factory every day of her life from the time she was sixteen until she keeled over at the sewing machine on her sixty-third birthday." Susan sighed, absently rubbed her belly. "I miss her almost as much as I miss my mom. They were both very special women."

"It sounds like it." Jarod brightened. "So besides your sisters, you have aunts, uncles, cousins?"

"Well, I have two surviving aunts, and three cousins. We exchange Christmas cards, an occasional letter. We're not terribly close."

"Why is that?"

"There was a falling-out between my mother and my aunts many years ago." The memory was hazy but painful. "Divorce was considered a cardinal sin in my family. When my mother divorced my father, her family pretty much disowned her."

"I'm sorry to hear that. What about the rest of your family?"

"That's pretty much all that's left of it. One of my uncles died in Korea. The other had a heart attack when he was fifty, and my mother's youngest sister died in childbirth, when she was barely nineteen." Susan shook her head, rubbed her eyelids with her fingertips. "Enough of this stroll down memory lane. Why are you so interested in my genealogy?"

"Because your relatives are also the relatives of my child. Of course I'm interested in them."

"You really are taking this biological imperative seriously, aren't you?"

A flush of anger spread across his jaw. "Bringing a child into the world is considerably more than a biological imperative. It's a lifetime commitment. I'd think you'd realize that."

She smiled. "I do realize that. I'm happy to know that you do, too."

"I thought I'd already passed your damned fatherhood test."

"This was merely a pop quiz to hone your skills."

"My son hones my skills every day."

"Yes, he does do that, doesn't he?" Her chuckle faded as she remembered the original direction of conversation. "Which brings us full circle. Why did you refer to our child as her? Was it wishful thinking, a slip of the tongue, or do you know something I don't?"

Jarod glanced around the cramped apartment as if seeking something else with which to change the topic. "Interesting afghan you have on the sofa. Handmade, isn't it?"

"You requested gender identification, didn't you?"

He pursed his lips, shifted his stance. "They already had samples of amniotic fluid. The lab simply used some to determine the sex of the child."

"At your request."

"Yes, at my request."

"Did it occur to you that I might not want to know in advance, that I might want to be surprised?" Try as she might, Susan couldn't seem to work up a healthy resentment. In fact, she was annoyed that she hadn't thought of requesting gender results herself. Her tone softened. "We're having a baby girl?"

Jarod smiled, met her gaze. "Yes. A daughter."

"Wow." Susan felt the silly grin slide across her face, and didn't fight it. "I've always wanted a little girl."

"Me too."

She regarded him. "I thought men only wanted sons."

"Sons are great, but daughters…" He sighed, grinned. "Haven't you ever heard the term *daddy's girl?*"

"I've heard the term and envied it. I always wanted to be a daddy's girl. Unfortunately, that requires the presence of a daddy to begin with."

His smile faded. "I can't believe any father would turn his back on you."

"Believe it." She moistened her lips, glanced away. "Not that I took it personally."

"Of course you took it personally. Children take everything personally. Danny is still convinced that his mother died because he spilled cereal on the kitchen floor."

That both startled Susan and broke her heart. "Why would he think that?"

Jarod turned away, but not before Susan saw the agony in his eyes. "You'd better get ready. We'll lose our reservations if we're late."

"Jarod—"

"Don't." He raised a hand, palm out, as if blocking the direction of her thoughts, and the question he correctly perceived was balanced on the tip of her tongue. "Don't ask about my wife's death, Susan. Please, just don't ask."

Something cracked inside her chest. His grief shattered her. "I'm so sorry. I didn't mean to intrude."

"It's something I'd rather not talk about."

"I understand."

He wiped his face with his palms. "I've made a mess of this, haven't I?"

"Of what?"

"This…" he gestured as if encompassing the entire room, and everyone in it "…us, the baby…all of it."

Because her knees suddenly began to tremble, Susan sat carefully on the arm of an upholstered chair. "We made an impulsive choice that now has consequence. Both of us made the choice, Jarod. We're sharing the consequence."

"My share pales in comparison to yours." He hesitated, regarded her with great thought. "I'm not an easy man to live with, Susan. I know that. I understand why you wouldn't want to spend the next few months under my roof, tied to me as my wife even in name only. All I can do is promise you that I'll try to make this difficult time as easy as possible for you, and for our child. I'll provide whatever you need and try not to intrude upon your privacy. Our daughter needs a family, Susan. She does not need to begin her life as a mistake."

Tears leaked into Susan's eyes. She brushed them away, unwilling to allow Jarod to see how deeply touched she was. "This child will never see herself as a mistake. I won't allow it."

"Neither will I." He took a breath, let it out. "Please marry me, Susan. For the sake of our child."

A lump wedged in Susan's throat. She whispered around it. "Yes, Jarod, I'll marry you."

Even as she spoke, a voice whispered in the back of her mind that her decision would change not only the course of her child's life, but of her own as well. Jarod Bodine was a man Susan could fall in love with. That made him dangerous.

And it scared her to death.

Chapter Seven

The rusty watering can was nearly obscured by a pile of discarded fence posts and a tangled tuft of dead saw grass. Dented but serviceable, the spouted container was exactly what Susan needed.

Delighted by her discovery, Susan used a spigot beside the porch ramp to fill the can, then nearly fell over when she tried to hoist the darned thing. Either five gallons of water was heavier than she remembered or pregnancy had sapped her strength. Regardless of the reason, she found herself staggering toward the wilting flower garden, heaving the sloshing can forward with each step to use the weight as momentum.

A cooling shadow alerted her barely a moment before the heavy burden was plucked from her grasp as if it weighed no more than an empty wicker basket.

She stumbled back a step, shaded her eyes. ''Good

grief, do you always sneak up on people? You nearly scared the life out of me.''

Jarod regarded her without a trace of contrition. ''Lifting isn't good for you.''

''Neither is a heart attack.'' She touched her throat, waited for her pulse to normalize.

In the two days since they'd stood before a bored magistrate and exchanged perfunctory vows, she'd barely seen her newly acquired husband. Jarod left before dawn, returned well after dark to reheat the supper Martha had tucked in the microwave for him. Their only conversation had been polite platitudes in passing.

Not that Susan blamed him for avoiding her. Their situation was so unique, so achingly awkward, that neither seemed willing to confront the harsh realities of it any sooner than necessary.

Now she straightened, absently rubbed a stubborn ache in the small of her back and glanced around the complex, wondering where a broad-shouldered hulk of a man could lurk without being noticed. ''Where did you come from, anyway?''

''A willing egg and a happy sperm,'' he replied without the trace of a smile. ''Next time the flowers need water, tell Martha. She'll do it.''

''How nice of you to volunteer her. I'm sure she'll be pleased, as bored as she must be with all the free time she has after having cleaned two homes and cooked for two families every day.''

A muscle in his jaw twitched. ''Are you comfortable?''

She blinked. ''Excuse me?''

''In the guest room.'' He shifted, glanced away. The sun gleamed on a tiny white scar at the edge of his chin. "I wish you'd taken the master bedroom, as I suggested. It's more spacious."

"I don't need much space."

"It also has a private bath."

"I don't need a private bath."

"Is there anything you do need?"

"Nothing, thank you." Susan wondered why she'd never noticed that tiny chin scar. It was irrationally sexy. She didn't know why. "I'm quite comfortable."

"The mattress isn't too firm?"

"I like a firm mattress."

"The closet isn't too small?"

She managed a wry smile. "Since most of my wardrobe will soon be relegated to long-term storage, there's more than enough room to accommodate the few garments I own that can be coaxed around an expanding waistline."

His gaze dropped to her midsection, which had swollen enough to stretch the fabric of her T-shirt. "You'll need some maternity clothes soon. There's a box of Gail's things in the attic—"

"No!" Susan sighed, shifted, planted one hand on her hip and used the other to wipe her face. She had no idea why the idea of wearing his deceased wife's clothing was so upsetting to her. "I mean, that's very kind of you, but it won't be necessary."

Jarod studied her without comment, then carried the watering can over to the garden and set it beside the vine-covered plow. He bent to pluck a small weed from between a pair of thirsty marigolds. Holding the tiny stem between his thumb and index finger, he scrutinized the weed as if it were a fascinating anomaly rather than one of a thousand hearty sprouts now invading the colorful plot.

"Gail wouldn't mind," he said finally. "She was a very sharing person."

Susan felt about two inches high. Her strident response had made her seem incredibly shallow and ungrateful. "I know. From what I've heard, she was a warm, wonderful woman."

"Yes." Jarod flicked the weed away, brushed his palms together as if trying to remove all traces of it. "She was very special."

"Tell me about her." The rash words were blurted before Susan could consider the consequence.

A flicker of pain flashed through his eyes, tightened his lips and drove a dagger into Susan's heart. "Why do you want to know?"

A good question. She had no rational answer beyond an intrinsic need to understand what kind of woman this man, this very special individual to whom she was now married, had once cherished and loved beyond measure.

"Her essence resides here," Susan said carefully. "I see her vibrance in her choice of colors, the items she arranged to display a delightfully zany sense of decor. I see her image in her son's face, her kindness reflected by the loyalty of her friends, her loving nature enshrined in the pain you still feel at her loss. It's natural to be curious about someone who has so deeply affected those around me."

He considered that. "Yes, I suppose it is." He lifted the watering can, used his sleeve to wipe caked dirt from the perforated sprinkler head before emptying the contents into the thirsty garden soil. "You can make any changes you want to the house. New furniture, new paint, new doo-dads to decorate the place."

Susan wobbled in place for a moment, then wiped

her palms on her oversize shirt, and walked toward the garden just as Jarod emptied the watering can.

Despite being unnerved by his offer to allow her free reign with any misplaced nesting instinct she might possess, the fact that he'd avoided answering her question about his deceased wife did not escape her notice. "That's very thoughtful of you, but your wife obviously loved the house just the way it is. I wouldn't feel right changing anything."

He leveled a gaze at her. "Gail doesn't live here anymore. You do. It's your home now. You have a right to be comfortable in it."

"It's only my home temporarily."

A frown puckered his forehead beneath the crown of his battered old hat. He glanced at the house, as if assuring himself they weren't being overheard. "We agreed not to discuss that."

"Actually, we didn't agree upon anything. You simply informed me that our arrangement was to be kept from Danny, because you decided, quite on your own I might add, to deceive him about the true nature of our relationship."

The comment clearly perplexed him. "Why would you be angry because my son was so thrilled about our marriage that I didn't have the heart to tell him it was just a temporary arrangement, that the baby sister he's ecstatic about won't even be living under the same roof with him?"

She flinched, recalling her own uncomfortable conversation with Danny, in which she'd tried to explain why she'd married his daddy, but slept in the guest room. She'd taken the easy way out, muttering some incomprehensible drivel about pregnant women thrashing about and keeping long-suffering husbands awake all night. The child had seemed to accept that. For now.

"I'm not angry, Jarod, but children need to trust what their parents tell them. There are consequences to withholding the truth. Remember the ghost-horse nightmares?"

For a split second, Jarod froze, then he blinked and continued to study the sprinkling water as if it was the most fascinating sight on earth.

"What did Danny say when you told him that Thunder was still alive?"

Jarod silently watched the final drops of water drain from the can.

Something in his gaze sent a chill down her spine. "Jarod? You did tell him, didn't you?"

After an excruciating moment, he straightened, balancing the empty can with a single finger wrapped around its handle. "I told him."

"And…?"

"And he asked me if I liked Thunder more than I liked him."

"Oh." Susan's stomach dropped to her toes. "He was just looking for…reassurance."

"Yeah. Reassurance." The misery in his eyes leaked through a calculated snap of anger. "My son actually needed reassurance that I loved him more than I loved a damned animal. What kind of father does that make me?"

"The very fact that you ask that question already implies the answer." Susan stepped forward, laid a hand on his forearm. His muscles quivered at her touch, and her own fingertips tingled as if they could feel the warmth of his skin, the tickle of fine hairs hidden beneath his sleeve.

He blinked, his gaze dropped to her hand, pale against the chambray work shirt. She thought she heard the sharp intake of his breath, but finally decided she'd imagined it because he didn't appear to be breathing at all.

Certainly Susan wasn't breathing. Air backed into her lungs, held there by invisible fingers until her chest felt as if it would explode.

Suddenly, she exhaled all at once, heard the sound of her own voice float firm on the warm air, drowning out the raucous call of a nearby jay. "Being a good parent doesn't mean your children will never be insecure, needy or frightened. Such emotions are natural in youngsters struggling to comprehend their place in the world. All children need understanding, patience, the reassurance that they are not only loved, but are also worthy of that love. You give your son that, Jarod, and you give him so much more. You care about him, care about his secret feelings and his fragile self-esteem, you nurture his hopes and soothe his fears. You aren't just a good father, you are a great one, a shining example on which your own child will model his own parental role, as will his children and his children's children. That's what kind of father you are, Jarod, and it is a noble legacy indeed."

The front of his shirt shuddered, as if his lungs were struggling to expel captured air just as hers had done. When he exhaled, it was slow, cautious, with a wary whisper of a sigh. He moistened his lips, tore his gaze from hers with apparent difficulty. "If you believe that, then you'll just have to trust that I know what's best for my son. At the moment I believe it's best that he believe our marriage, our family, is permanent and stable."

It took a moment for Susan to realize that she had backed herself into a semantical corner from which there seemed no logical escape. Her shoulders sagged in defeat. "I just wish you hadn't found it necessary to lie, that's all."

"Wishes are free." Jarod took the empty can over to the spigot to refill it. "Everything else costs money. Speaking of which, your name has been added to my credit card accounts. Feel free to use them to purchase anything you need for the house, for yourself or for the baby." He straightened, ignored her stunned stare, and carried the watering can back to the garden. "I'll put a hose on that spigot tomorrow, one long enough that you can water the weeds behind the barn if you want to. You shouldn't carry anything heavier than a bag of sugar."

His tone annoyed her. She managed a smart salute to enforce her miffed glare. "Yes, sir, Captain, sir. Would that be a five-pound bag of sugar or the fifty-pound bag Martha keeps in the pantry? Just wondering, because I wouldn't want to violate the orders of He-Who-Is-in-Charge."

He spared her a glance. "Hormones."

"Excuse me?"

"Pregnancy makes the hormones wacky. That's why you're so cranky."

"I am *not* cranky."

He tossed the empty watering can aside, tipped back his hat and squinted toward the stables. "Gail threw a mug at me once when I suggested she give up her morning coffee because caffeine wasn't good for the baby."

"Did you duck?"

"Yes."

"Pity."

He grinned. "That's exactly what she said."

"Don't even think about asking me to give up coffee."

"I wouldn't dream of it. That lesson has been well-learned."

"Then you aren't completely hopeless."

"You didn't think I was so hopeless when we—" His teasing smile faded, and a crimson flush crept up his throat.

Feeling bold, Susan finished the sentence for him. "When we spent the night together in a cheap motel." The misery in his eyes tugged her conscience. "I'm sorry. That sounded snide, and I didn't mean it that way."

"I know." He gently took her elbow, guided her toward the path leading up to the stables. They walked in silence for a moment, then he stepped in front of her, grasping her shoulders. "I'm not the kind of man who hangs out in bars looking to pick up women."

His fervency startled her. "I never thought you were."

"Good. That's…good." He looked slightly relieved, but unconvinced.

A thought struck her. "What about me, Jarod? What opinion did you form about my presence there?"

"You told me you'd gone to hear the band and drown your sorrows because the man you'd been involved with wanted a more permanent relationship than you did and decided to marry someone else."

She flinched at the reminder. The man in question had been a staid, decent fellow. Susan had been extremely fond of him. He'd wanted marriage, a home, a family, all the things that practical, pragmatic Susan had determined were mere fantasies in the harsh reality of a world where marriage was merely a temporary respite between divorces.

"Yes, that's what I told you. Did you believe it?"

"It was what I wanted to hear."

"But did you believe it?"

He considered the question longer than Susan found comfortable. Finally, he released his grip on her shoulders and tucked his thumbs in his pockets. "Not at first. Later, after we'd, uh, talked..." the scarlet flush along his throat deepened, "...I realized that you were probably being honest."

"Probably?"

He shrugged. "We'd spent twelve hours together. How much can anyone really know about another person in twelve hours?"

The question rocked her back on her heels, not because it was complex, but because it was so deceptively simple. Her response was a thin whisper. "Not much, I suppose." She moistened her lips. "Strangers in the night, exciting, erotic, arousing, then a bittersweet goodbye and a glorious memory. Exquisitely romantic until reality scuffs up the shine."

Jarod's eyes took on a sudden shine. "Was the memory glorious, Susan?"

She stepped back, absently clutching the modest opening at her collar. The question made her feel exposed, vulnerable. Was the memory glorious?

Was the sun warm?

Was water wet?

The memory of that night still haunted her, still made her skin tingle, her pulse race. Every nuance of scent and sweetness, of gentle whispers and caresses so tender she'd nearly wept with sheer joy, every kiss, every touch, every gasp of wonder was forever etched in her mind. And in her heart.

That was what frightened her, made her feel so emotionally exposed. Susan didn't believe in love at first sight. She didn't believe in love, period. At least not the romantic kind. The love between parent and child, between siblings, between caring friends, that was something wholly different than the breath-catching, gaze-locking, passion-erupting desire that passed as love, but which Susan considered to be nothing more than natural biology.

Until she'd met Jarod, a man who attracted and annoyed her with equal aplomb, a man whose scent made her thighs quiver, whose smile made her heart go all flumpy, a man with a sexy little chin scar that her lips positively ached to kiss.

In the sunlight, his eyes weren't just a nondescript shade of gray. Below the thin shade line cast by the rim of his hat, his eyes sparkled with flecks of brilliant blue, shone with silvery iridescence. She saw passion in his eyes, the same passion she remembered from the night they were together. The same passion now boiling up inside her with a frenzy that frightened her.

Her pulse throbbed, her skin tingled, a peculiar buzzing invaded her ears. Every nerve was alive with electric excitement. This man, this unique and special person affected her in ways she could never have imagined.

The buzzing grew louder, more persistent. She vaguely noticed, but was too mesmerized by his gaze to pay much attention. He was, she decided, the sexiest man on the face of the planet. At that moment, as she stood beside a split-rail fence beyond which spirited horses grazed and galloped, Susan was overwhelmed by a desire far beyond her scope of experience. She wanted him more than she wanted her next breath.

Their gazes were locked, melded, fused as if by magic. For only an instant, his glance fluttered to the side. He lifted a hand slowly, deliberately, reaching toward her as if to brush away an errant strand of hair.

"Don't move," he whispered.

Susan wouldn't have moved if her sneakers had been on fire. She wanted him to touch her, caress her. She wanted him to kiss her, then sweep her into his arms and carry her to his bed. She wanted to experience all those deliciously erotic wonders her frivolous, romance-ridden sisters had giggled about during teen-aged flights of fancy. Susan had scoffed at their silliness.

She wasn't scoffing any more. It was all she could do to keep from tearing his clothes off and mounting him where he stood.

Jarod's fingertips brushed her hair. A tingle of excitement shot from her scalp to her toes. "Hold very still."

"Uh-huh." Not the most intelligent uttering, although it was the best she could come up with considering that her full attention was riveted on his mouth, on lips that should have been too sensual, too tender for a man, but were surprisingly suited to the intricate angles of features that were undeniably masculine.

She remembered the feel of those lush lips, remembered the heat, the flavor, the incredible power—

A shiver raced through her. She turned up her face, parted her lips, and waited for a kiss that never came.

Instead she felt a slight tug on her hair. When she opened her eyes, Jarod turned away from her, shook his closed fist, and flinched as if in pain. A moment later he flung a crushed yellow jacket to the ground.

Jarod ground the crumpled corpse under his boot heel, then regarded Susan anxiously. "Are you all right?"

She managed to find her voice, or at least a croaking facsimile of it. "Yes." She reached for his hand, turned it palm up and cringed at the pulsing venom sacs attached to his skin. "You've been stung."

Not that he needed her to relay such information. He was no doubt aware of his predicament, since his entire arm probably felt as if it were on fire. Susan had once been stung by a common honeybee, and had thought at the time she was going to die. She'd heard that yellow jacket stings were a hundred times worse.

Taking a deep breath, she carefully withdrew the stinger from his flesh and could have wept at the angry red welt in his palm. "Why didn't you just swat it away or something?"

The question seemed to startle him. "It was tangled in your hair."

"But you deliberately let it sting you."

He frowned, flinched slightly and stared down at his palm, flexing his fingers as if assuring himself they still moved. "It's not a big deal."

"No one has ever slain a yellow jacket for me before."

A subtle smile tilted the corner of his mouth. "I'm lucky there aren't any dragons in Montana."

"If there were, would you slay them to protect me?"

"With my bare hands," he whispered.

And she believed him.

* * *

The pain in his hand was nothing compared to the agony in his loins. He wanted her. Dear God, he'd never wanted anything in his life as much as he wanted this woman with the soft green eyes, the golden hair rustling in the breeze, the delicate curve of throat that begged for a man's kiss.

This woman who was his wife.

His wife.

The memory of Gail's features flickered through his mind, along with a stab of guilt so acute it nearly doubled him over. He'd stood over her grave weeping and had promised that he'd never marry again.

Now he'd betrayed her, betrayed the memory of a woman who had endured isolation without complaint, concealed loneliness with a gentle smile, and had self-lessly devoted herself to her family despite a secret unhappiness that Jarod had pretended not to see be-cause he hadn't known how to alleviate it.

Jarod had loved her deeply. In the end, that love had destroyed her.

He'd vowed to himself that he'd never marry again, never subject another woman to his unworthiness as a husband, never open his own heart to such devastation and pain. It had been a vow ripped from his very soul.

Now he stood as if rooted to earth that was as much a part of him as the blood in his veins, and felt his vows crumbling into dust.

Physical desire was a fleeting thing. Jarod under-stood biology, the mating urge that propelled all living things into reproductive frenzy. He could deal with such urges, painful as they might be. He could control them. He *would* control them.

Emotional entanglement was another matter, the quest of an empty soul, the squeeze of a still-raw heart. Susan touched Jarod on a level too deep for tears, soothed a place inside him that he'd walled off not only from the world but from his own prying mind.

She was an enigma, this beautiful woman with the pretense of tough independence shrouding a bruised and tender heart. Jarod wanted to scoop her into his arms, shield her from the ugliness of a reality she didn't yet understand. He wanted to protect her, to cherish her. He wanted to love her.

But he wouldn't. God help him, he couldn't. Love was a destroyer of souls. Jarod's was already gone.

Chapter Eight

Jarod's pickup rumbled up the dusty driveway toward the Roundtree ranch, then pulled into a grazing pasture beside a dozen other vehicles. A cacophony of laughter and cheerful voices floated through the closed truck window.

Susan was so nervous she feared she might be sick. She tugged the front of an oversize T-shirt that hung loosely enough to cover both her swelling stomach and the unfashionable elastic waistband of the only slacks she owned that could be coaxed over her burgeoning figure.

Despite the warmth of the late spring day, she also wore a long-sleeved shirt, left unbuttoned, to add another layer of concealment. "I'm not sure this was a good idea."

"Good or not, we are expected." Jarod flipped off the ignition, slid a warning glance past the excited youngster seated between the two adults. "The Roundtrees are holding this shindig in our honor. It would be rude to have refused their invitation."

"Wow!" Danny shifted, flattened his palms on the truck's bench seat and pushed himself upward to get a better view through the windshield. A half-dozen laughing children were scampering around the pasture playing kickball. "Look, Joshua and Tyler are here! They'll get to sign my new cast!"

The child's excitement brought a smile to Susan's lips, and offered the perfect excuse to avoid eye contact with his somber-faced father. "You'll get lots of autographs today, I'm sure, but you'll have to be careful." She fondly brushed a tousled lock of hair from his face. The post-operative cast had been replaced by a lighter version that increased his mobility, and allowed him to use crutches. "Don't overexert yourself."

"I won't." He glanced at Susan with an expression too pensive for an eight-year-old. "Can I call you Mom?"

The question stunned her. For the past two weeks Danny had clearly been thrilled by her presence, had routinely reached out to hug her for no reason, and she'd frequently seen him watching her with a huge grin. He hadn't called her anything, however, had merely begun his conversations by diving directly into the heart of the matter. She was flabbergasted by the request, instantly worried about how Jarod would react.

Words stumbled to the tip of her tongue and stuck there. "I...uh..."

A glance at Jarod confirmed that he'd gone rigid and was staring out the windshield as if he'd been chipped out of stone. The only perceptible movement was a twitch at the curve of his jaw.

Susan forced a smile. "This seems an odd time to ask such a thing, Danny."

The boy frowned, more out of exasperation than annoyance, Susan suspected. He was a child who anticipated instant answers and immediate gratification. "My friends will make fun of me if I call you Miss Mitchell, and Dad says it's not polite to call grown-ups by their first name."

She acknowledged the point with a stiff nod, a thin smile. "Nobody will ever take your mother's place, Danny. You know that, don't you?"

He gave no indication of having heard her. "Joey Vasquez has a stepmother, and he calls her Mom." Danny squirmed impatiently. "Are you gonna let me out of the truck or what?"

"Hmm? Oh. Of course."

Nerves twisted her stomach as Jarod exited the vehicle without comment. As for Danny's question, Susan decided that it had been a thinly veiled pronouncement in disguise. No matter what her response had been, the boy had already made his decision. Susan was secretly thrilled.

Mom. Such a beautiful word from a child she loved as much as if he'd been her own. And she did love Danny, loved him so much it frightened her.

The passenger door opened. A grim-faced Jarod chivalrously helped Susan step down, avoiding the question in her gaze. She wondered if he was hurt by Danny's request, if he felt it a betrayal of his wife's memory.

The question would have to wait. As Jarod lifted his son from the truck cab, Martha strolled toward the parking area with a smiling, dark-haired woman Susan had never met before.

The woman rubbed her palms on a pair of well-worn blue jeans before extending her hand to Susan. "I'm Lorraine Roundtree. Welcome."

Susan regarded the woman, whose dark eyes shone with curiosity and good humor, and said, "It was kind of you to invite us."

Lorraine's handshake was extraordinarily firm and warm, her laughter high-pitched, rather shattering in an infectious, grin-evoking kind of way. "Now it wouldn't have been much of a wedding party without the bride and groom, would it? 'Course, it's a few weeks late, but hey…any excuse to chill the beer for an old-fashioned potluck, eh, Marty?"

Martha's lips quirked. "Aye, and since when have the Roundtrees needed a reason to party?"

"Hush, now. You don't want to give Mrs. Bodine the wrong impression of us, do you? Why, she's liable to think we're all just a bunch of hard-riding, hard-drinking, saddle-sore cowpokes with dung on our boots and straw between our teeth."

Martha issued a good-natured snort.

Susan, feeling more relaxed already, laughed. "Why on earth would I think that?"

"Mostly because it's true." Lorraine slid her a teasing wink, then emitted another ear-shattering guffaw that startled a yellow hound napping in the shade of a ramshackle shed. "Come with me, hon. I'll introduce you to some folks. Most ain't worth knowing, but since neighbors are few and far between out here, you might as well learn who to watch out for."

Susan shot a glance back to see Jarod retrieve

Danny's crutches from the pickup bed. "Sounds ominous."

"Oh, it is." Lorraine cupped a chummy hand around her elbow, propelled her toward the frightening crowd. "We'll start with the worst of the lot. Hey, Lou! Come meet the new Mrs. Bodine!"

A huge, meaty-fisted man swung away from a group gathered around an elongated table filled with cakes and casserole dishes. He clutched a beer in one hand, tugged the brim of a peculiar feathered fedora with the other. "What the hell you bothering me for, woman? Can't you see we got some serious man-talk going on?"

Lorraine gave him a gesture usually frowned upon in mixed company. "Get your lazy butt over here before I kick it halfway to Wyoming."

"You ain't near big enough to kick my macho beehind, lady."

"Come here and try me, you thick-headed fool."

"Them's fighting words."

Lorraine balled up her fists, took a boxing stance, sniffed and thumbed her nose at him.

Lou let out an indignant roar, kicked dust, stomped across the ground like an angry bull. "You done it now, gal."

"Oo-o-o, I'm scared, I am."

Stunned, Susan tottered back a step, her gaze darting around the crowd of happy party-goers, none of whom seemed to be the slightest bit interested in the fact that their hostess was intentionally provoking fisticuffs with a burly, red-eared cowboy who looked strong enough to crack a fence post with his teeth.

Still snarling, the cowboy thundered toward the petite, dark-haired woman standing her ground with a gloating grin. When he reached her, he snarled, pulled her into his arms, and kissed her with enough fervor that even onlookers must have felt the heat. Susan sure as heck did. The passion of their embrace weakened even her knees.

Martha, who'd shaded her eyes with her hand and had been perusing a group of men gathered outside the old barn, favored the smooching pair with a glance. "At it again, are they?"

Susan blinked, swallowed hard. "Uh…"

"Try throwing a bucket of water on them," Martha said mildly. "It doesn't work, but 'tis great fun."

It was the first hint of humor Susan had ever seen in Jarod's stoic housekeeper. Martha had always been polite but had also kept her distance, seeming to be wary of Susan's presence in the house. Since Martha and Gail Bodine had been close friends, it seemed prudent not to press the issue, although Susan would have enjoyed a more amiable relationship with Martha, whose loyalty and devotion she admired.

Susan wondered if it would distress Martha to hear Gail's son call another woman Mom.

The question would have to wait, because Lorraine finally tottered back with a satisfied sigh, gave Susan a mischievous smile. "This here is my husband, Lou. Lou, this is Jarod's new missus."

The ruddy face that had been so frightening only moments ago now split into an incongruously elfin grin. He stuck out a hand the size of a dinner plate. His grasp, Susan noted gratefully, was gentler than his wife's. "Glad to meet you, Mrs. Bodine."

"Please, call me Susan."

"Sure thing, Susan. That's a right pretty name." The man nodded, his eyes sparkling with intelligence and homespun humor. "It's good Jarod finally found himself a fine woman to warm his bed. He's been cranky long enough, if you ask me."

Lorraine snorted. "Nobody did ask you, you fat-skulled, muscle-bound, mush-for-brains studmuffin."

Lou's thick eyebrows puckered into what Susan now recognized as a fake frown. "Put a sock in it, you loud-mouthed, sweet-lipped, nagging hunk o' burning love."

Lorraine purred deep in her throat. "Take me, big boy."

"I, uh…" Susan managed a weak smile. "It was nice meeting you. I think I'll hunt up that water bucket now."

"Oh, no, you're not getting away that easy."

Chuckling, Lorraine blew her husband a kiss, grasped Susan's hand, and spent the next twenty minutes alternating introductions with bawdy tales that frequently flummoxed or embarrassed Susan, but more often kept her burbling with guilty laughter.

Susan recognized most of the children from her intermittent stints as a substitute teacher for the local elementary and middle schools. She'd also met some of the parents during the annual back-to-school night, when the classrooms were opened for the children to show off school projects to the community at large.

The ambiance of that setting had been pleasant enough, but there had still been a polite reserve about the townsfolk, a sense of non-inclusive courtesy that had reminded Susan of her outsider status.

Now some of the same people who had regarded her with coolness and mistrust were pumping her hand with genuine enthusiasm or wrapping her in a startling bear hug without seeming to notice that her stomach reached them before the rest of her.

Susan was accepted. Not because she had performed her function as educator with admirable aplomb, although she was an excellent teacher. No, she was being welcomed with open arms simply because she was now a Bodine.

If she'd ever doubted Jarod's power in the community, she had only to see him as he was now, surrounded by those who clearly regarded him as a respected paragon. When he spoke, all chatter ceased, and his every word was heard with measured consideration. He was clearly respected, treated with the reverence of a tribal elder, a beloved chief.

From her vantage point inside a circle of women discussing wild game recipes, Susan studied Jarod in his natural element.

"If the government prohibits grazing on public lands, we'll all flop belly-up bankrupt inside of a year," one sad-eyed man said.

A fellow with a scraggly gray beard and a wad of stringy, shoulder-length hair tied at his nape shuffled forward. "Well, ain't nobody gonna tell me I can't run my cows where my pappy and grandpappy ran theirs."

"I heard the guv'ment was gonna claim private ranch land, make the whole damned state a national park or sumthin'."

"They try that, and someone's gonna die."

Several in the group nodded. "Yep, got me a load of buckshot for anyone who tries to steal what's mine."

"What do you think, Jarod? What should we do?"

A hush fell over the group. All eyes turned toward

the broad-shouldered man who was quite clearly their leader.

Jarod spoke quietly, without the emotional rancor expressed by others in the group. "The bill has been tabled until the next session of Congress. Our state legislators are already working on riders to exclude private land from the environmental provisions and to subsidize revenue loss from withdrawal of grazing rights." He paused, absently tilted the brim of his hat against the shimmering sunshine. "I've been thinking we should form a coalition with the national beef industry to analyze how the current public lands legislation will affect future food costs."

"That there's a good idea, Jarod."

"Yup, yup, real good idea."

One fellow scuffed the toe of his boot into the dirt, scowled from beneath his brimmed hat. "The guv'ment's got no business telling me how to run my cattle."

Jarod shrugged. "We are the government," he said quietly. "We've got a say in how things are run, but no bigger say than anyone else in this country. Life changes. We have to change with it. Whatever happens, we'll work together, we'll adapt and we'll survive."

A rumble of relief circled the group, followed by a round of raucous laughter when one of the men cracked a slightly off-color joke.

Susan continued to study the interaction, continued to discover nuances of this unique man to whom fate had drawn her. Even when Jarod smiled, his eyes were somber, his countenance taut, wary. He didn't relish his position as leader, she realized, although he clearly understood it and accepted the responsibility bestowed upon him by virtue of his heritage.

But there was a price to be paid, a big one. Jarod was alone in a crowd, emotionally isolated by burdens he'd never requested but wouldn't refuse.

The harshness of that reality struck her with astounding force. For the first time, Susan understood something profound about Jarod Bodine, about his life, his heartaches, about the stoic silence with which he accepted them. He was a man on display in his own community, unable to remove the mask of invincibility for fear of revealing any weakness, any vulnerability that might shatter the tenuous hierarchy of the tribe.

There was no room for error, no time for grief, no place for solace in the life of a demi-god, a man whose every move rippled with economic consequence for an entire community. And when the loneliness became too agonizing, when the burdens were too heavy to bear, such a man faced his mortality alone, in a darkened pub a hundred miles away, wrapped in the arms of a stranger.

A stranger who had then become just one more burden that must be borne. Stoically. Quietly. Alone.

"So then he says, 'what'll ya give me for it?'"

Guffaws at the punch line startled Jarod from his mental reverie. He automatically laughed, much to the delight of the proud fellow who'd just told six jokes in a row, five of which Jarod hadn't really heard.

As was his habit during social occasions, Jarod was running on automatic pilot, absently rearranging his facial features from pleasant to amused to concerned by instinctively mirroring the context around him. His mind, however, was a whirl of thought, plans, processes. And worries.

He slipped a glance toward the pasture where several youngsters still scampered playing kickball. Danny, who'd initially been surrounded by excited peers anxious to make their mark on his cast, had been abandoned now and watched from the sidelines, tottering on crutches that weren't designed for use on uneven, outdoor terrain.

Jarod suppressed an urge to retrieve his son, and cart him off to a nice, safe chair where his infirmity would be pampered and catered to. The boy looked so forlorn, so abandoned. So alone.

A dart of sympathy stuck square in Jarod's chest. It was a tough lesson in reality, one he wasn't quite ready to see being thrust upon a child so young.

Still, his son was old enough to have claimed Susan as his own, bestowed upon her the most cherished of intimacies. Danny regarded her as a mother-figure. His mom.

The power of that still shook like a fist in Jarod's soul. Another mother for his son to love. And to lose.

The ramifications of his decision to wed Susan had spiraled beyond anything he could have imagined. The true reason for that decision was still wrapped tightly, locked in a secret part of his heart. Someday he might find the courage to peer inside that private place, perhaps glean an understanding of the nature of a man.

Someday. But not this day.

As Jarod watched, Danny shifted on his crutches. His small chest heaved in what was probably a sigh of boredom, or perhaps the annoyance of a slightly spoiled youngster unaccustomed to relinquishing his usual role as center of attention.

With some effort, Jarod turned away. He felt a prickle of warmth on his face, instinctively glanced toward the source and locked his gaze with Susan, who was staring right at him.

The unexpected eye contact startled her. She blinked, went pale. When she turned her face away from him, sunlight gleamed from the moisture on her cheek.

She was crying.

Jarod's chest tightened as if it had been wrapped in barbed wire. He couldn't breathe, couldn't move, was paralyzed by shock and a pain so intense that it nearly buckled his knees.

She was crying.

"So what do you think, Jarod? Should we start us a petition drive or—"

The voices circled like annoying insects, questions, comments, demands. He heard all of it, he heard none of it. His mind, his heart, were focused on the fragile tears of a woman he'd cared for more deeply than he dared acknowledge, a woman whose heart he had broken, whose life he had ruined.

"Something wrong, Jarod?"

"You ain't looking too good."

"Needs him a beer, that's what."

Commanding his feet to move, Jarod strode across the dusty ground, ignoring both the startled comments from the circle of men and the surprised glances from the women gathered nearby.

Susan lowered her gaze as he approached, brushed a breeze-tangled strand of hair from her face while discreetly wiping the moisture from her cheek. Jarod nodded to the curious women, slipped a protective arm around his wife's shoulders, and walked her away from their neighbors' prying ears.

He led her to a fenced pasture where wild mustard and lupines grew. Voices from the party-goers dissolved into a distant buzz, mingled with laughter from the children playing kickball in the field beyond the barn.

Grasping her shoulders, he turned her toward him, slipped a knuckle under her chin to raise her face. She didn't resist, but kept her gaze averted.

"I'm sorry," he whispered. "I'm so very, very sorry."

Her eyes widened suddenly. She looked straight at him, gazing so deeply that he wondered if she could actually read his soul. "Sorry for what? For being a man that others look up to and depend upon, for being so honorable that your own happiness is constantly set aside for the good of others?"

He didn't know exactly what he'd expected her to say, but that wasn't even close. Bewildered, he opened his mouth, only to close it when no sound emerged. He swallowed, cleared his throat, tried again. "I'm sorry that I insisted that we come here today. I didn't realize how unhappy it would make you."

She blinked. "I am not unhappy."

"You're crying."

"Yes."

"Crying means unhappiness."

"Sometimes." She took a shuddering breath, reached up and brushed a silken fingertip along the small scar he'd gotten falling off the barn roof as a child. "Sometimes it's just an expression of emotion."

Her touch made him shiver, sent a frisson of electricity through every nerve in his body. "So you are weeping because you're having such a wonderful time?''

She smiled, a soft, gentle tilting of her lips that made him quiver inside. ''Actually I *am* having a nice time. I like your friends. They've made me feel very welcome.'' Her smile faded, her eyes darkened to the emerald hue of a summer pond. ''I've just realized how much of yourself you conceal for the sake of others. They depend upon you because they understand that you will always be there for them, that they won't wake up in the middle of the night and find your closet empty.''

Now it was Jarod's turn to blink. ''I don't know how folks do things in the city, but out here we don't generally check out our neighbors' closets. It seems a tad rude, actually.''

A pink flush colored her previously pale cheeks. She shrugged, tried for a self-deprecating smile that didn't quite come off.

''You're talking about your daddy, aren't you?'' Jarod studied the flicker of pain in her eyes. ''Did you wake up in the middle of the night and find your daddy's closet empty?''

''Yes.'' It was a whisper. ''It was my stepfather, actually. My real father left when I was tiny.''

''What happened with your stepfather?''

She glanced away, her gaze distant. ''I was barely five, but I remember it as if it happened yesterday. I remember talking to my baby sister in her crib, trying to explain that it wasn't her fault, that men simply left when they got tired of being fathers because that's how men were. Even though Catrina was only a few months old, it never occurred to me that she was too young to feel pain and to remember it.'' A fresh glim-

mer of tears deepened the verdant glow of her eyes.
"That's why I was so certain that Danny could recall
details about his mother, even though he was very
small when she died. There are things that alter a
child's life so profoundly that the memory is imprinted
forever, even without the maturity to actually understand what has happened."

Her pain affected Jarod in ways that frightened him.
He wanted to gather her in his arms and kiss away the
hurt, to make her smile again, to make her laugh with
delight, purr with sensual passion, and to erase the
painful memory of all who had ever wounded her.

Instead, he opened his mouth and stupidity fell out.
"That's too bad."

She flinched. "I didn't mean to be insensitive by
making a comparison between the death of a beloved
mother and the desertion of men who never wanted to
be parents in the first place."

"Damn, I ought to be shot." Frustrated with himself, Jarod shook his head, muttered an oath under his
breath. "I meant that you shouldn't have had to go
through that. No child should. I can't imagine what
kind of man could betray and abandon his own children. My father would have given his life for me or
my mother, and done so without a second thought. If
he had ever walked out, just left us as if we meant
nothing to him, I don't know what I would have done.
It would have shattered me. I can't imagine it, I just
can't imagine it."

"I know," she whispered. "That's what makes you
so special."

"I'm not special. Every man here today would take
a bullet to protect their family."

She smiled. "Taking a bullet is easy. Hanging around, spending a lifetime, that's difficult."

"Not when it's where you want to be."

Her smile faded. "How about when it's not where you want to be, but where your honor tells you that you must be?"

For the first time, Jarod had a glimmer of understanding about what this was truly about. "I want our baby, Susan, want her very, very much."

"I know you do." Tears spurted, ran down her cheeks. "That is what makes me cry."

Helpless, upset, totally befuddled, Jarod awkwardly dabbed the wetness with his thumb. "Well, damn it all, that makes no sense at all."

"Pregnant women aren't supposed to make sense, remember? It's those pesky hormones." She managed a thin laugh, which faded as she gazed up at him. "Our daughter will be a very lucky child to have you as a father. Even though the pregnancy was an accident neither of us expected, has added burdens you do not need and a wife you never wanted, I simply can't be sorry it happened."

Jarod's legs quivered. He locked his knees, fought to stay upright.

A wife you never wanted.

Quiet words, spoken without rancor or emotion. Words that he could not dispute, since neither of them had ever pretended the marriage was anything but a legal nicety to protect their unborn child.

No, Jarod's shock wasn't in hearing the words spoken aloud; the shock was in suddenly realizing that despite his pretense to the contrary, it wasn't true, had never been true. In his heart, in that secret place he'd never dared look, he had wanted Susan to be his wife from the first moment he'd laid eyes on her.

. . And that truly terrified him.

"It's magnificent." The grateful whisper caught in Susan's throat, a lump of pure emotion around which she could barely speak.

Beside her, Jarod took a corner of the intricate, hand-sewn wedding-ring quilt and nodded toward Lorraine Roundtree, and the grinning ladies who had created the gift. "We thank you kindly," he said.

"Glad you like it," Lorraine said. "If you think that one's nice, wait until you see the fancy frills the sewing bee is aworking up for your new young'un."

Susan's head snapped around, her jaw drooped in horror.

Lorraine's grin instantly flattened. "Oops."

Astounded by the revelation, Susan couldn't have uttered a sound if her life had depended upon it.

To her relief, Jarod stepped up, slipped his arm around her shoulders and broke the strained silence with a cheery chuckle, and an exaggerated drawl. "Hell, if only half the county knows about it, it's still a secret. Now y'all keep this to yourselves so the two or three fools who haven't read the announcements posted up in the general store don't find out until we're good and ready to tell 'em, y'hear?"

Laughter rumbled around the group, which instantly dispersed back into its male and female circles, each buzzing happily among itself.

Lorraine hurried forward, pried the quilt from Susan's rigid fingers and folded it back into its bag. "Honey, I'm so sorry. I knew you wanted it to be kept quiet and all, but it just kinda slipped out."

Susan licked her lips. "The entire town knows?"

"Well, mostly." Lorraine angled a glance at Martha, who merely shook her head in annoyance. "It's not like we're busybodies or anything, but babies are a pretty big deal around here. We're right fond of them, so we figure anyone who starts wearing a T-shirt on the outside instead of tucked in is pretty much making an announcement. That's how we do things around here. Subtle, you know?"

Martha snorted again. "Aye, 'tis as subtle as a stud with a willing mare." She strolled over to Susan, touched her forehead with the back of a cool hand, and regarded her with concern. "Tuckered out, are you? You're looking a wee bit peaked."

"I'm fine," Susan murmured, realizing that this was the first personal interest Martha had ever taken in her. "The truth is that I was nervous about coming, but I couldn't be happier that I did. I feel like I've made new friends here today."

"You didn't make new friends," Lorraine said cheerfully. "You just got a chance to meet some that you already had."

Susan chuckled. "Oddly enough, that makes sense. Thank you."

Lorraine glanced over her shoulder. "You were right, Marty. She fits right in—"

The scream of terror shattered every nerve in Susan's body. She froze for what seemed a small eternity, but was in reality no more than a heartbeat. Conversation instantly ceased. Every head turned, every eye focused on the pasture where the children had been playing.

A horse whinnied, hooves beat hardened earth.

There was another shriek, a heart-wrenching wail that ripped Susan's heart out. "Danny," she croaked.

Jarod was fast. Susan was faster. Despite her thickening belly, she spun on her heel, sprinted around the barn and saw what she feared most. Danny was crumpled on the ground, tangled in his crutches, alternately screaming and sobbing wildly as two adolescents on horseback struggled to control their nervous mounts.

"Get those animals away from here!" Jarod shouted.

One of the riders, a girl who appeared to be about thirteen, reined in a snorting chestnut mare. "We were just racing for the creek, like we always do. The horses spooked when he started hollering."

Lorraine huffed up, her olive skin paled to a sickly ochre. "I told you, no riding today. Didn't I tell you that?"

The girl bit her lip. "Yes, Mama."

"Both of you, get down and walk those animals back to their stalls. Wipe them down, then get yourselves into the house and wait for me. You are in such trouble."

While Lorraine scolded her children, Susan darted toward Danny, gathered the sobbing boy into her arms and rocked him as if he were a toddler. "Shh, sweetie, it's all right. Everything is going to be all right."

Jarod anxiously squatted beside them. "Are you hurt, son?"

The boy shook his head. "I—I—" he hiccuped, sobbed "I hate horses, I hate them all." He took a shuddering breath. "I wish they were all dead."

From the corner of her eye Susan saw the life drain from Jarod's eyes. His pain pierced her heart. She hugged Danny, brushed a kiss across his mussed hair.

"I know you feel that way now. It's okay to be scared and angry. Someday you'll feel differently."

"No, I won't. I hate them." He was shaking so violently it frightened her. "I hate horses, I hate ranches, I hate Montana. My mom hated them too. That's why she died, so she wouldn't have to be here anymore."

Jarod looked as if he'd been shot. He sat back on his heels, swayed slightly, then stood, tugged his hat down to his eyebrows. He gazed across the prairie toward the distant mesas, blocks of barren beauty rising from a rippling plain as if absorbing strength from the land.

Pale anguish shrouded his eyes, a depth of sorrow beyond pain, beyond any agony of the heart that she could possibly comprehend.

In that moment, Susan suddenly understood that Danny's hurtful words were more than the echo of a frightened, angry child. Danny actually believed what he'd said, but that wasn't the worst part.

The worst part was the stunning realization that Jarod believed it, too.

The sorrowful song of crickets filled the night air. Filtered moonlight sprayed between clouds darker than a devil's soul. A storm was coming.

The screen door creaked as Susan pushed it open. Behind her, it rattled shut. She rubbed her chilled arms, wandered across the porch to where Jarod leaned on the railing, gazing out toward the stables.

She propped her hip against the baluster, studied the darkness to envision the vistas the night concealed. "Danny finally fell asleep."

Jarod nodded. "The horses are restless tonight. Samuel said Buttermilk is off her feed."

Susan had wandered to the stables on occasion. She enjoyed bringing carrots and other treats to the horses, so she knew that Buttermilk was a beautiful golden mare with liquid fudge eyes and a sweet disposition. The stable hands had also told her that Buttermilk had been Gail's favorite. From what Susan had been told, Gail hadn't been much of a rider but had developed a bond with the gentle, brown-eyed mare.

Danny had also learned to ride on Buttermilk, although he'd been promised that Thunder would be his as soon as he was old enough to handle the spirited mustang. Unfortunately Danny wasn't a child who appreciated limits, and he routinely stretched allowable boundaries with predictable results.

"I've always loved horses myself," Susan said. "When I was a little girl, I always asked Santa to bring me a pony for Christmas."

"Did he?"

"No, he never did. My mother said it was because there wasn't enough room in our apartment." Susan smiled. "Now I just look out the window and see the horses prancing the paddocks. It's like Christmas every day. I wish I knew how to ride."

"After the baby is born, I'll teach you."

A frisson of excitement skittered, then faded. She looked away. After the baby was born, Susan knew she'd be moving back to town, and Jarod, who wore fatherhood like a second skin, would become one of those sad-eyed weekend parents for whom he had previously expressed pity.

She licked her lips, shoved the unhappy thought into

a far corner of her mind. "I would love that. Perhaps I could learn on Buttermilk, just like Danny did."

"Probably not on Buttermilk." Jarod pushed away from the porch rail, folded his arms across his chest. "The Roundtrees have been trying to buy her for years. Her lineage would complement a young stallion they've been wanting to stud."

"You're going to sell Buttermilk?"

"The Roundtrees would do right by her, wouldn't over-breed her. She's young enough to give them several good foals, then they'd spoil her rotten for the rest of her days."

"But this is her home."

He frowned, shrugged. "She's just a horse. All she cares about is a warm stall, a green pasture, and a bucket of oats once in a while."

"If you believe animals are so intellectually deficient, why did I hear you explaining to Claude why he couldn't use the sofa as a scratching post?"

Jarod blinked. "You eavesdropping on my conversations now?"

"Aha, so you admit you were having a conversation with a cat."

He glanced glumly toward the stable, where a shaft of moonlight illuminated the white split-rail fencing of the adjoining pastures. "The Roundtrees need a good broodmare. I happen to have one. That's the way life is on a ranch. Animals come and they go. You treat them with kindness and respect, but you don't get attached to them."

"Interesting philosophy." She studied the angles of his face, shadowed by a fleeting shaft of moonlight. "It's a steaming pile of what the hands shovel out of the horse stalls every day, but it's interesting nonetheless.''

Only the quirk of his brow implied that he'd heard her.

''You adore your animals, Jarod. Every one of them is special in your eyes.''

He neither confirmed nor denied it. In fact, he said nothing at all, just continued to stare into the darkness with a shuttered gaze.

''Are you planning on selling all your horses because of Danny's fear?'' she asked. ''Because if you are, it would be a mistake. Fear is temporary. Danny will overcome it eventually.''

''Maybe.'' He paused, as if choosing his words. ''But animals are living beings. They need care and attention. Buttermilk needs more attention than most. She's used to having Danny bring carrots to her, groom her, ride her. She's lonely now, feeling sad and abandoned. That's not fair to an animal that can't be expected to understand the intricacies of human emotion. The mare deserves to be in a place where she is loved, appreciated, given the attention she deserves.''

Jarod's empathy touched Susan. ''Perhaps you shouldn't make that decision yet, not until Danny has had an opportunity to make his feelings known.''

''Danny has already made his feelings known.'' He slanted a quick glance, then looked away. ''In more ways than one.''

She moistened her lips. ''Did it upset you when Danny asked if he could call me Mom?''

Jarod's jaw twitched. ''It surprised me.''

''But did it upset you?''

He considered for a long moment, then replied without looking at her. ''Yes, I suppose it did.''

"Because it seems a betrayal of his mother's memory?"

The question clearly startled him. "Gail wouldn't have considered that a betrayal. She wasn't that selfish." Jarod took off his hat, wiped his forearm across his brow. He sighed, replaced his headgear. "Danny loves you. You've been able to touch something deep inside him, something I could never quite reach. That would have made Gail very happy. Danny deserves to love and be loved."

It was all she could do to keep from caressing his face. Her fingers itched to touch him, her arms ached to hold him. Such a stoic man and yet so tender inside. "And what about you, Jarod? Do you deserve that, too?"

A flash of fear kindled, then died. He turned away without reply, but not before she recognized the look in his eye. It was the same expression she'd seen earlier that day, when Danny had sobbed that his mother had decided to die so she wouldn't have to live here anymore.

"Children say outrageous things sometimes," Susan said quietly. "Especially when they are angry or scared. They don't really have a concept of abstract thought, and they confuse their own muddled feelings as everyone else's reality." Bewildered, Susan laid her hand on his arm, felt the taut muscles twitch at her touch. "I don't know how to talk to Danny about this, Jarod, I don't know how to help him, because I don't understand what happened myself. Martha won't talk about it, nobody else seems to know anything."

Stepping aside, Jarod moved away from her touch, turned his face into the darkness, and spoke with a chill that froze her to the core. "Danny has convinced himself that his mother died because she didn't love him enough to live. The truth is that she died because I didn't love her enough to save her.'' He looked over his shoulder, impaled her with a gaze. ''Tell me, Susan, how will my son be helped by knowing that?''

And with that stunning question, Susan's world collapsed.

Chapter Nine

Shock reverberated through Susan's body, a quiver of stunned disbelief that trembled upward from her feet and settled in her horrified eyes.

Watching her stunned comprehension twisted every nerve in Jarod's body. He kept his voice bland, a stark contrast to the raging turmoil of a wounded soul. "You might as well know what kind of man I really am, Susan. I take advantage of people. I seek out their weaknesses, use them to further my own needs no matter what the cost."

She shook her head slowly, denying the reality even as she took a tremulous step backward. "I don't believe that."

"The truth doesn't require your validation." Something cracked deep inside him. He knew he was going to offer Susan the freedom he'd denied to Gail, even though it meant he would lose her. Jarod hadn't realized how much the loss would hurt. "You want to know why Danny hates this place, Susan? Why he blames it for his mother's death? Because he can't bring himself to place the blame and hatred where it belongs, on the shoulders of the only parent he has left."

Susan studied him for a moment, her eyes luminous in the moonlight, but suddenly unreadable. "Gail died of pneumonia. That much is common knowledge. What bewilders me is why people whisper her name in hushed tones, as if something sinister had happened when her death was clearly a tragic circumstance for which no one can possibly be blamed."

Miserable, Jarod silently cursed himself for having allowed the probe into his heart to go so far. He didn't want to discuss this, didn't want to remind himself of how bitterly he'd failed a woman whose only crime was loving her family more than she'd loved herself. "Gail's death was a culmination of a lifestyle she'd never wanted. Folks who knew her realize that."

"I don't understand. Are you saying that you some-how forced Gail to marry you the way—" Susan bit off the words, glanced away.

Jarod finished her question. "The way I forced you to marry me?"

She sighed, rubbed her eyes. "Nobody forces me to do anything. You made a very strong case for the le-galities of the situation, and I eventually agreed with you." Folding her arms, she propped a hip against the porch rail and met his gaze. "Since you've already mentioned how difficult it was to conceive Danny, I have to presume that your relationship with Gail was considerably different. She was under no pressure to marry you beyond the obvious one."

"The obvious one?"

"That she loved you deeply and wanted to be your wife."

For some reason, those words stung because they were a subtle reminder that Susan did not love him and had not wanted to be his wife. He didn't know why that thought distressed him so.

"Gail and I grew up together." Jarod spoke slowly, concentrating on a roughened patch of peeling paint on the porch post. The tackiness surprised him. He hadn't noticed how he'd let the place go since Gail's death, as if maintaining a pristine environment no longer mattered. "We were sweethearts all through high school. Everyone just assumed we'd get married, have a family, and run the ranch just as my parents had done and their parents before them. The problem was that Gail had other dreams for her life. None of them included pulling calves with a come-along at two in the morning and watching the family checkbook drain into the business account just to keep the herd alive during winter."

He sighed, glanced away from the peeling paint long enough to cringe at Susan's incredulous expression. "I'm worth a lot of money, of course, but the bulk of it is tied up in land, equipment and animals."

"Are you saying that you honestly believe you weren't rich enough for her?"

"No. Gail never cared about money."

"Then I'm totally confused."

"Yeah." He sighed, wished he didn't feel so irrationally compelled to explain the unexplainable. "Gail hated ranching, hated Montana. Danny was right about that. She always dreamed of living in an exciting city bustling with people. Even as a kid she talked about moving to New York City and becoming a famous designer.'' He paused, glanced over and saw the perplexed pucker of Susan's brow. ''Gail was a pretty good artist and an excellent seamstress. Designing fancy clothes was her thing. She loved that stuff, absolutely loved it.''

Susan pursed her lips, nodded. ''Her artistic perceptions were unique. The decor of the house reflects it. Danny clearly inherited his talent from her.''

''He sure didn't get any of it from me. I can't draw a straight line with a ruler.'' Jarod absently flicked a crawling night beetle off the porch rail. ''Anyway, I never paid much attention to her clothing designs beyond a few condescending remarks about her cute little hobby. Then she was offered a design scholarship at some fancy college in San Francisco.''

''Oh.''

The impact of that single word made Jarod cringe. ''I'm sure you can figure out where this is leading.''

''I presume you didn't want her to take the scholarship.''

''Hell no, I didn't want her to take it. That wouldn't fit into my plans, my needs. I didn't much give a damn about hers.''

The bitter edge on his voice seemed to shock Susan, but she remained silent. She simply stood quietly, expecting him to continue.

After a moment, he did. ''I told Gail I wouldn't wait for her, that if she took the scholarship we were through. So she gave it all up, married me and was miserable ever after.''

The memory shattered him anew, a pain as exquisite as if he was reliving it all over again.

''Gail hated the isolation.'' He spoke quietly, as if

speaking only to a soft night and a forgiving God. "She hated the loneliness. She never complained, but I knew how unhappy she was. I just never had enough time to deal with it. The ranch had problems, more important problems than those of an unhappy woman who just happened to be my wife." There was no rancor in his voice, just exquisite sadness. "I was working long hours to increase production, cut costs, scrape together a small fortune to buy even more acreage to support a bigger herd. I thought it was what was expected of me, to leave a larger legacy than the one I inherited."

Susan tilted her head, regarded him for a moment. Jarod expected her to spit on his boots and walk away, but she didn't. Instead she reached out, laid a gentle hand on his arm.

It was a soft touch, a warm contrast to the cool night air, but with an impact more powerful than a punch. Understanding seeped from her sweet palm straight into Jarod's soul, a loving gesture that humbled him, shamed him, yet made him want to weep with gratitude.

"Tell me the rest," she murmured. "You don't need to carry this burden alone."

He shook his head, stared at the slim hand on his arm, pale in the moonlight, so sweet he wanted to clutch it between his palms and kiss each fingertip until the void inside him was filled with her goodness. He didn't want to share the guilt, the shame. He didn't want her to know what kind of man he really was; yet it was too late for deception. Any illusions she'd held about his stoic goodness had already been shattered into dust.

"It was calving season," he heard himself say.

"Colder than a normal spring. The snow melt was slow, the grazing was poor, a large percentage of the herd went farrow that year. There had been too many miscarriages during the winter. The springers that had made it through were having trouble. Too many still-births, too many weak calves, too many sick mommas. There was enough work for a hundred men, but I tried to cut costs by working half that many twice as long. Samuel was so tuckered he threatened to quit. I wouldn't listen. I worked twenty hours a day and expected everyone else to do the same."

The words floated as if from outside himself. Jarod heard his voice, knew he was speaking, but found himself listening as if it were a story being told by a stranger.

"That's when Gail got sick. She said it was just a virus, maybe the flu. I wanted her to go see the doctor, but she said it wasn't bad enough. Since that's what I wanted to hear, it didn't occur to me that she was actually too sick to attempt a sixty-mile drive to the only medical facility in the county. And, of course, she'd never have inconvenienced either her husband or her friends by asking them to take her."

The porch post really was a mess, Jarod thought. Some of the balusters would have to be replaced, and the entire structure would have to be scraped and sanded for paint to adhere. Not that it mattered. Soon there would be nobody around to care that the house, the ranch, and Jarod's own life had fallen into a shamble of disrepair.

Only the ghosts of those he had disappointed.

Only the ghosts.

Jarod heard his own voice, a calm, rational voice revealing none of the inner chaos that twisted inside his wounded heart. "A sensitive man wouldn't have needed a request for help. But then, I've never been particularly sensitive unless it suited me."

From the corner of his eye, he saw her turn away. Shadows veiled her expression, but not before he recognized her flinch of despair. Susan removed her hand from his arm, glanced away, gazing toward the stables as if unwilling to look at him. He didn't blame her. But the loss of her calming touch grieved him.

The voice that was his took on a peculiar quiver. "During that time, I was rarely home before midnight, always up before dawn. One morning Gail felt a little warm to me, so I woke her up to make sure she was all right. She said she was fine. That's what I wanted to hear, of course. Gail always told me what I wanted to hear."

There was no rancor in the peculiar voice-that-was-his-own. Only a profound sorrow, a tremor of emotion ripped from the core of his soul. "It was almost 2:00 a.m. when I finally got home that night. Danny had fallen asleep on the sofa. The television was on. There were cereal bowls on the kitchen table, milk slopped everywhere. I knew at a glance that Danny had gotten his own breakfast, and probably had had cereal for lunch and dinner as well. I rushed into the bedroom. Gail was burning up with fever, gasping for breath. I bundled her and Danny into the truck, drove like a madman. By the time we reached the hospital, she was gone."

The night was silent, deathly silent. No chirp of crickets, no croaking toads, nothing but the rush of his own blood pounding past his ears.

Beside him, Susan was also silent, seemingly mesmerized by the bleak darkness beyond the dim glow

of the porch light. He longed to touch her, to slip his
fingers into the silken strands of her hair and take solace from the softness.

Her shoulders quivered. She bowed her head and
her hair spilled forward, obscuring the shadowed edge
of her face.

Jarod spoke. "So now you know."

"Yes." A whisper in the night, thin and tremulous.
"Now I know." She raised her head with a flip that
shifted the hair from her face, turned slowly to face
him. A glimmer of moisture traced the curve of her
cheek. "I know that you and Danny suffered a tragedy
of immense proportions, an anguish that I cannot even
begin to comprehend. I am so very, very sorry for your
loss."

He studied her eyes for blame, for disgust, for a hint
of disdain. There was none. He thumbed the moisture
from her cheek, stunned to realize the tears were for
him. "Gail died because I wasn't there for her."

"Gail died because she was very sick."

"If I'd taken her to the hospital that morning, she'd
still be alive."

Susan gave his point momentary consideration. "Is
it easier for you to believe that than to accept the fact
that there are things in this world beyond your control?"

He lowered his hand to his side, would have stepped
back if the porch rail hadn't dug into his hip. "Control
has nothing to do with this."

"Doesn't it?" There was no accusation in her eyes,
only sympathy and understanding. "Death is such a
cruel master. It strikes without warning, without our
permission. How frightening it is to realize that we
cannot cocoon those we love to protect them from its

grasp. It is a terror beyond comprehension for most of us, so we simply pretend that if we are careful enough, if we are sufficiently vigilant, we can keep death at bay.''

Susan paused, rubbed her upper arms in a gesture that appeared to be a delaying tactic rather than a response to the cool night air.

When she spoke again, her voice was thin, but composed. ''We relentlessly guard our children, as of course we should. We monitor our food, our exercise, our health. We convince ourselves that we can outfox our own mortality until we make a conscious decision to leave this place and seek out another. But despite all we do, accidents happen, sickness happens, death happens.''

She paused again, gauging his reaction.

Jarod could only shake his head. The emotional impact of her words had shaken him into silence.

''It's not your fault,'' Susan whispered. ''It wasn't Gail's fault, either. She didn't choose to die because she was unhappy here. Don't be angry with yourself—'' she paused a beat ''—or with her.''

Jarod's upper torso snapped around. He stared at Susan, stunned by a pronouncement that was too simple to be true, too true to be ignored.

Because beneath the grief, beneath the guilt, beneath a sorrow too deep for tears, Jarod recognized the anger, searing anger. Anger that Gail had left him, left their son.

And when he peered into that dark, hidden recess of his heart, a dreary place within himself that he'd dared not explore, he recognized the agonizing belief that Gail had deliberately chosen death because Jarod had failed her as a husband.

* * *

"It's all right," Susan murmured.

She studied the anguish in his eyes, saw the remorse, the flood of bereavement that had been swallowed up by guilt, wrapped, tied and spirited away to a secret hiding place. Something cracked deep inside her. She regretted having discovered that hiding place, regretted having opened the package of pain. Her own guilt at having done so struck like a halberd to her heart.

"I'm sorry," she whispered. "It wasn't my place to—"

He touched a fingertip to her lips, silencing her. "No. You were right. I've never really dealt with... with what happened. And I've never helped my son deal with it, either."

"You will." Susan's knees trembled, her breath caught in her throat. His fingertip still rested against her mouth. She kissed it softly, caught it between her lips and was rewarded by his sharp intake of breath.

Although he made no move to pull away, she cupped his hand between her palms, nuzzled each fingertip with delicate sweetness. All the yearning, all the secret desire she'd bottled so tightly inside her spilled forth in a burst of passion that would have shocked her if she hadn't been too overwhelmed to think clearly.

He whispered her name like a question, like a prayer. For a moment she feared he would spurn her. She wouldn't have blamed him. The timing could not be more inappropriate.

Nor could it be more perfect. It was so natural, so totally natural. He stood naked before her, emotionally stripped, all pretenses discarded, all secrets revealed. He had displayed himself, his vulnerabilities.

Susan had never felt closer to another human being in her entire life.

She wanted this man, wanted to hold him and be held by him, to comfort and be comforted, wanted to cherish each moment of life as if it were the last. There was something profound about the eventual acceptance of one's own mortality, a desperation to live for the moment that blotted out temperance in a burst of sudden passion. Each breath was a gift, each day of life a joy that could never be recaptured. To look back in regret, that was the truest sorrow.

The first time Susan had impulsively discarded her pragmatic reality, she'd enjoyed the most magnificent experience of her life, and now she carried the seed of that wonder in her swelling belly. This man had the ability to slip past emotional barriers, ignite passions far deeper than mere sexual desires. With Jarod she felt a bonding of souls, a sweetness beyond anything her pragmatic existence had ever imagined.

Drained, shaken, overwhelmed by emotions that she couldn't define or identify, Susan squeezed her eyes closed, pressed her face into Jarod's warm palm. "I don't want to be alone tonight." Breath shuddered out, weakening her knees. "I don't think you want to be alone either."

He took a sharp breath. "I'm not strong enough."

"I don't understand."

A breeze fluttered around her face, ruffling her hair. He gently brushed the errant strand away, then cupped her cheek with his palm. "Don't you realize how you affect me, Susan? Your footsteps in the night torment my body, just as they torment my mind. My strength wanes every time your scent lingers in the hall, or I glimpse a scrap of lingerie draped over your bed, my gut tightens and I feel like I might explode. I keep remembering what we shared, the beauty, the passion. Some nights it's all I can think about.''

"I think about it, too," she whispered.

"Do you?" There was an intensity to the question, a croaking desperation that startled her. "Was what we shared...special to you?"

"It was very special."

"But you said you regretted it."

"So did you."

"I lied."

"So did I."

They stared at each other for a long moment. "I won't deny that I want you. I'm a man, not a saint."

"I'm counting on that." Emboldened, she danced her fingers along the waistband of his pants. "I hear that saints make boring lovers."

He hesitated, but made no move to restrain her seeking fingers. "I don't want to take advantage of...our situation."

"That's very noble of you." She circled her fingertip around the metal fastener of his jeans. "I, however, am not so magnanimous. I do want to take advantage of our situation. I want to take advantage of you." A flick of her wrist, and the waistband opened a notch. "What do you think of that, Mr. Bodine?"

He swallowed hard, moistened his lips. "I rather like the idea, Mrs. Bodine."

"I'd hoped that you would." Susan couldn't believe that husky, teasing voice was actually emanating from her. She sounded so alluring, so sexually confident. Nothing could be further from reality. Here she was, pretending to be a svelte, sensual seductress when anyone with eyes would see a disheveled pregnant person with a protruding stomach, bloated ankles, and a heat rash under her chin.

Yet Jarod continued to gaze at her as if she were the most desirable female on the face of the planet. "You are an incredible woman. I've never known anyone like you."

"I'm one of a kind," Susan whispered. A flush of heat rose up her throat, burned across her jaw. "That isn't necessarily a good thing."

"Oh, it's a good thing." He bent to kiss her forehead, whispered against her brow. "It's a very good thing."

She lifted her face to him, and he found her mouth with his lips, possessing her with a kiss so tender, so achingly beautiful that she feared she might faint from sheer joy. She felt as if she was floating, as if her feet would never touch ground again. When his lips moved to sip the corners of her mouth, she sighed. "I'd forgotten how good you are at this."

"Hmm?" He nipped at her earlobe, traced a moist line down her throat. "Good at what?"

"Don't taunt me. You know what." She shivered. The man could melt the quills off a porcupine with his kiss. And that wasn't all he did well. The memory sent shards of electric anticipation shooting down her spine. "You're making me crazy."

"I want to make you crazy." His whisper brushed the quivering pulse at her throat. "I want to make you gasp and cry and call out my name when the tremors shake you to the marrow. I want to touch every inch of your body, marvel over the softness of your beauty, the warmth of your soul. I want to bury myself deep inside you, touch places you never even knew existed. I want all of that, Susan, and I want it so bad it scares me.''

She sagged against him as her knees buckled. ''Then take it, Jarod. Take it all, and take me with you.''

Scooping her into his arms as if she were weightless, Jarod shifted the screen door open with his elbow and carried her into the house.

It was the embodiment of a secret dream, the covert illusion of her youth, when she'd scoffed at the romantic notions of her dewy-eyed sisters, only to conceal the same hopeless daydream hidden deep inside her own heart. The Cinderella syndrome, she'd called it, the weakness of her gender to yearn for a knight in shining armor galloping on a noble steed to make life complete. A false fable, a flawed fantasy.

Or was it?

Susan's knight wore scuffed boots with denim armor. He was dazzlingly knight-like, straddling one of the proud animals from his stable, although his steed of choice guzzled gasoline not oats. But had he made her life complete?

The question swirled through a dizzied mind vaguely aware of its surroundings. Susan realized she was being carried through the dimly lit living room. Indistinct sound simmered from the stereo, music so soft it was barely a vibration of tempo and of mood.

The hallway closed in on them. The door to the master bedroom loomed ahead. And the question reasserted itself with more vengeance.

Had Jarod Bodine made her life complete?

Susan had been content before she'd met him. Most

of the time she'd actually been happy, happy with her job, with herself, with her life.

Jostling her in his arms, Jarod shouldered the bedroom door. It swung open with a quiet creak. He stepped inside, paused for a moment, his breath coming in ragged gulps.

"Put me down," Susan whispered. "I'm too heavy."

"No heavier than a feather in the wind." A clever tilt of his face brought his mouth down on hers.

Her resistance melted, her blood steamed. Every fiber of her being cried out for attention, the tender, sweet, exquisitely erotic consideration that she remembered from their last night together. Vaguely aware that he had lowered her feet to the floor, she clung to him with irrational desperation. Her arms encircled his neck, her fingers itched to tangle in his hair but had to fight the barrier of his hat.

With a growl of annoyance, she snatched the headgear off, flicked it away.

He broke the kiss with a smile, but his lips still hovered a breath away from her own. "That was my lucky hat."

"Its job is done, cowboy." She traced her fingertip along the edge of his fly, and felt the quiver of his arousal. "You are about to get incredibly lucky."

Stunned by her own boldness, she unzipped his pants, peeled the fabric back to expose that which tantalized her. Cotton briefs were now the only barrier between her seeking fingers and his pulsing masculinity. In a flash of sudden nerves, her mouth went dry. She pulled her hand back, lowered her gaze. "Was I this forward the last time?"

"I think I took the lead then." He took her hand, pressed it against himself. "Now it's your turn."

His heat seared into her palm. "I suddenly feel rather shy." She managed a weak laugh, then felt like crying for no good reason beyond an immediate terror of removing her own clothing, and exhibiting a body that was not in its prime. "Odd, modesty has never been much of a problem for me."

"So I recall."

A teasing glint lightened his tone, although Susan felt herself flush at the memory of how she'd ripped her own clothing off before Jarod had even managed to step out of his pants.

He stroked her brow, kissed the top of her head with great gentleness. "Would you like to change into something more comfortable?"

"That's the oldest line in the book."

"Only because it yields excellent results."

She studied the buttons on his shirt, fiddled with one of them until it came off in her hand.

He stared down at the plastic disk in her palm. "That's one way of doing it, I suppose."

"I'm sorry."

He took the button, tossed it over his shoulder, then deliberately ripped his shirt open, popping most of the remaining buttons off in the process. "You're right. This is much more efficient. But for m'lady..." he grasped the hem of her tunic-sized T-shirt, teased her with a sexy smile, "...perhaps slow and easy would be best."

He lifted the garment, pausing as she raised her arms to allow him to slip it over her head. Dropping the cotton shirt, he turned his attention to her slacks. His thumbs traced the waistband from the small of her back around her sides and above her belly. He lowered the garment, kneeling as he did so and pausing to kiss her swollen stomach with a reverence that touched her to the quick.

Gently, tenderly, he caressed the distended part of her that protected their unborn child, pressing his face against her bare skin in a gesture of absolute adoration.

"You are so beautiful," he murmured. "So perfect."

Any doubt that he would still find her attractive dissolved in the golden glow of his gaze, an expression of wonder mingled with desire that melted her fears, left her trembling with joy. Again and again he kissed her belly while his palms cupped her buttocks with infinite care. Every brush of his lips, every stroke of his fingertips sent shivers of anticipation through every nerve in her body.

A fluid warmth seeped from deep inside her, a moist welcome anxious for his arrival.

When she was certain she could endure no more, he slipped her fragile panties down to her ankles, then stood and removed her bra. Her breasts sprang free, and he immediately cherished them with his fingers, teasing the nipples until they hardened like pink diamonds.

A moan of pleasure drifted from her lips. Her thighs quivered, her belly tightened with need. When he took one breast into his mouth, she grasped his shoulders to keep from collapsing into a puddle of passion.

She closed her eyes, rolled her head back and gave in to the waves of wonder washing over her body. Every caress, every touch was a fire in her veins. Every cell, every nerve, every fiber of her body was alive, pulsing with pleasure.

"Now," she heard herself whisper. "I want you now."

"Soon." His fingertips continued their lazy exploration undaunted. "Very soon."

Protest rolled to the tip of her tongue, only to be swallowed with a gasp as he stepped away from her. Cold air rushed into the gap between them, chilling her. Her eyes sprang open, and she watched in horror as he stripped off the rest of his clothing, gave her a dazzling grin, then spun and walked out of the room.

Tottering back a step, Susan foolishly covered her breasts with her arms. She felt naked, vulnerable and exposed. Of course she *was* naked, vulnerable and exposed. She was also alone.

But not for long.

Within seconds, Jarod returned, and spread the wedding-ring quilt over his king-size bed. "Our friends intended for us to share this gift," he said with a smile. "It's only fair that we oblige them."

All she could manage was a mute nod.

With two steps he crossed the room, lifted her into his arms and carried her to their marital bed. He laid her gently upon the quilted cover, then stretched out beside her. His palm slid from her shoulder to her flank, his gaze probed hers with deep reverence. "Susan—"

"Shh." She turned onto her side, touching her hand to his lips. "Tomorrow we'll talk. Tonight, no words are needed."

He studied her for a heartbeat longer, then pulled her into his arms, kissing her with a passion that left her limp and gasping.

They clutched each other with a desperation borne of silence, the passion of probing fingers and slickened flesh, and steaming heat rising in the dark. Their hands joined, fingers twined so tightly neither could tell where their own flesh ended and the other's began.

Tiny sobs rent the air, mingled with groans and gasps, and whispered cries of pleasure. He moved over her, slipped into her and found that secret place so deep inside that she'd never known of its existence.

He melded with her body and soul, and when they finally leaped into that passionate abyss, the pragmatic non-believer who scoffed at fairy tales and thought romance the realm of idealistic fools had fallen madly, completely, irrevocably in love.

In that gasping, breathless moment, Susan understood with stunning clarity that her life would never be the same. That frightened her.

And with good reason.

Chapter Ten

Moonlight brightened a few scattered clouds. The dark horizon would glow with dawn soon. Another sunrise, another day.

A day unlike any other.

Jarod turned away from the window, gazed down at the rumpled bedclothes and the curled form of the woman sleeping peacefully. Last night hadn't been a dream. It had mirrored his dreams, so many over the past weeks he'd stopped counting them. But last night had been reality.

They had consummated their marriage. They had consummated a lie.

Susan moaned in her sleep, as if she'd heard his thoughts and was alarmed by them. He sat on the edge of the bed, gently pulled the colorful quilt over her exposed shoulder.

When was it, he wondered, that his lust had been

replaced by something deeper, more profound? When was it that he actually began to fool himself about the reality of their relationship?

They had created a child together. That much was real. In creating that child, they had also fused a bond that would bind him and Susan for the rest of their lives. That too was real.

Both of them understood that destiny and accepted it, just as they'd accepted the legalities that had brought them to this time and this place.

Somewhere along the line, Jarod's intentions had evolved from chivalrous and determined to…to what? He didn't know. This woman, this unique and precious soul had changed him, had woven a thread of magic and sewn it directly to his heart. The man who had steadfastly vowed never to marry again, never to subject another woman to his own shortcomings as a husband, never to subject his own heart to such devastation, loss and emotional pain, now found himself breaking every promise he'd ever made to himself.

All too soon he'd pay the price for having betrayed himself and the memory of a woman who had made the ultimate sacrifice to his selfish needs.

Eventually Susan would leave and take their child with her. That had been their deal. Jarod had promised to let Susan go.

Now he wondered if that would be just one more promise he wouldn't have the strength to keep.

"Mom, Mom!" Using his cane as a pivot, Danny navigated the uneven terrain with the hopping swing-gait mastered since his final cast had been removed a few days earlier. "You gotta see this, Mom! There are bullfrogs in the cow pond! One of them is as big as Claude!''

Laughing, Susan glanced up from her chore of clearing the remnants of their tailgate picnic. ''A frog as big as a cat? I find that difficult to believe.''

The sweaty, grinning child hop-swung around the truck, steadied himself by leaning against the side of the pickup bed. ''No fooling, he is huge! All green and warty and stuff. When he jumped into the water, water splashed all over me.''

Susan followed the child's excited gesture at the wet splotches below the knees of his khaki pants. ''Oh my, that is definitely evidence of a frog-induced tidal wave.'' She snapped the lid on the leftover potato salad, placed the container in the cooler, and wiped her hands on the maternity smock that flopped like a tent over her enormous stomach. ''I simply must see this incredible, croaking hulk for myself. Lead on.''

Grinning madly, Danny pivoted on his cane and headed back toward an oasis of wild poplar trees and water reeds in the massive, ten-acre pond that was both watering hole for grazing livestock and backup irrigation for nearby alfalfa fields that were now being harvested as winter feed for the herd.

''There's a whole bunch of frogs in there.'' Danny was pink with excitement. ''They were all croaking and stuff until I got too close.''

Susan could hear a few deep-throated grunts from the creatures in question. Surprisingly loud, actually, not at all like the warbling ribbets of their smaller cousins. More like the vibrating rumble of a concrete truck, followed by the baritone screech of air brakes on a steep grade.

Oddly enough, Susan rather liked it.

Out of habit, she cupped her stomach with one hand as she walked, as if the gesture could actually keep the weight of her encumbrance from toppling her forward. Her breath came roughly as the growing child pressed upward into her lungs.

Although she exercised regularly and was in exceptionally good shape according to her duly impressed obstetrician, she tired more easily now. Even relatively benign physical activities frequently exhausted her.

Danny shot a worried glance over his shoulder, seemed relieved by the assurance that she was indeed following him. "Be real quiet, or they'll all jump in the water and swim away."

Since Susan's choices were limited to either speaking or breathing. She merely nodded, smiled and puffed forward a few more steps.

Behind her, the diesel harvester churned and creaked, its engine roar becoming louder as it chugged from the north end of the field, where Jarod was discussing the process with several ranch hands, to the south end toward the large pond where Danny was waiting.

As she approached the water's edge, the grinning youngster pointed toward a clump of cattails clustered at the shoreline. A rustle in the tall grass caught her ear. A moment later, a frog the size of a baseball suddenly hopped from the grass into the water with a plop and a splash.

Danny was beside himself. "Did you see it, huh, did you see it?"

"I did." Puffing, Susan braced herself on a poplar trunk, and longed for the good old days when she could have actually seated herself without the assistance of a forklift. "He was a handsome fellow, wasn't he? Not quite cat-size, but a significant amphibian nonetheless.''

Danny frowned. "Am-fibby-what?"

"Amphibian," came a masculine reply from behind Susan. "It's a fancy word teachers like to use when they mean bullfrog."

Before Susan could do more than turn her head, Jarod had slipped his arms around her, brushed a kiss against the back of her hair. "You promised that if I capitulated on this picnic thing you wouldn't exert yourself."

His warmth seeped right into her heart, loosing a surge of happiness so intense it nearly buckled her knees. Since the night they'd made love on their beautiful wedding-ring quilt, Jarod and Susan's relationship had evolved into a precious bonding that neither one of them could define. Nor did they try. Once Susan's tutorial commitments had ended and the summer school courses she taught were completed, she'd reveled in the time available to follow Jarod around, learning more about livestock and ranching than she'd ever believed possible.

Everything fascinated her, the magnificent animals, the beauty of the land, the immensely complex business of running a ranch that encompassed over a quarter of a million acres, including living quarters for a dozen people, a farming operation, a machine shop and repair facility, and an equipment yard that would be the envy of any public works director.

Through it all, Jarod had displayed great patience. He'd never been too busy to answer questions that must have seemed silly to him, or to explain business functions that were probably dry as Montana dust to a man who'd spent a lifetime incorporating them into his day-to-day life.

The more Susan had learned about that life, Jarod's life, the more impressed she'd become. Ranching was an exquisitely complex affair requiring the skills and knowledge of a dozen specialized professions from animal husbandry to meteorology, from cost-benefit financial analysis and long-term budget calculations to infrastructure, personnel and stock futures. It was no wonder that everyone in the county looked to Jarod for leadership, wisdom and guidance. He was not only a unique cross between cowboy and CEO, he was an exceptional human being as well. Susan was crazy about him.

She leaned back, thrilled by the exquisite warmth gilding her spine, the comfort of his strong arms encircling her. "I'm fine. I just wanted to see Danny's bullfrogs."

He nuzzled the curve of her neck. "Danny's bullfrogs will be around later, when you can visit them without tiring yourself."

"I'm not tired." It wasn't a lie, since she was suddenly energized by Jarod's presence.

Danny, who'd been squatting at the edge of the water, planted his cane tip in the mud and hoisted himself upright. "Dad, can we catch pollywogs?"

"Not today, son. I'm working."

A disappointed frown puckered the boy's face. "You're always working."

"Not always. Sometimes I take a hug break." To prove that point, he drew Susan closer, until her hips nested against his thighs and her back pressed his chest. "Have I told you lately how immensely beautiful you are?"

"Don't be cruel," she murmured, her attention riveted on the child who'd turned away with a resigned expression on his face. "I know I'm huge."

"You are perfect."

Susan bit her lower lip, studied Danny's rejected little form hunched over the edge of the water. "Why don't you spend a few minutes hunting pollywogs with him? It wouldn't take long, and you're already here—"

"There are no pollywogs." Jarod spun her around to face him, planted a kiss on her forehead. "They all sprouted limbs months ago, and now those aging, hormonal gentleman frogs are attempting to entice impressionable females into contributing to next spring's pollywog crop."

"Impressionable females?" She chuckled. "I'd think you'd have learned by now that females only pretend to be impressionable and allow males to believe they are in control simply for the sake of convenience."

"Oh, I'm well aware of the power of your gender, Mrs. Bodine." He nuzzled her neck. "God bless the fairer sex."

As much as Susan enjoyed the interlude, something she'd seen in Danny's eyes moments earlier still bothered her. She slipped another glance toward the boy, who'd turned away from the snuggling adults to redirect his attention into the murky waters of the pond. "Danny mentioned earlier that you brought him fishing here once."

Jarod's eyes widened. "He remembers that? I'm surprised. He was just a tadpole himself at the time. I fished, he just kind of sat on the bank and wet his diapers."

"He's been out of diapers a long time, Jarod."

Pride glistened in his gaze. "Yes, he's becoming a little man so fast."

"Children do grow fast. Too fast." She paused. "Why haven't you ever taken him fishing since he was a baby?"

A veil of caution slipped over Jarod's eyes. "He never mentioned that fishing interested him. There was always something else going on in his life. Baseball, soccer, riding—" He bit off the words, glanced away. "He seemed to prefer sports, that's all."

Susan saw the pain in his eyes. She touched his face, urging him to look at her. "It's normal that Danny is frightened of horses now, Jarod, but he may not always be. Give him time. He's not even completely healed yet."

Jarod nodded. "It's okay. I won't push him."

"I know you won't."

After a moment, he spoke again. "You've been so good for Danny. He's blossomed since you've been with us and is happier than he's been since before…" He glanced away, hesitated, then simply repeated, "You've been good for him."

A chill slipped between the edges of the compliment. Susan was acutely aware that Jarod had made a clear distinction between himself and his son. She adored Danny, loved that little boy as much as she loved the child growing in her womb. The fact that Jarod hadn't commented on her presence as being a positive effect on his own life didn't escape her notice.

Susan wanted to be good for Jarod, too.

"Dad, look!" Danny spun at the edge of the pond, gesturing wildly. "It's a catfish, a really big one, right there in the reeds!"

"A catfish, is it?" Jarod stepped back from Susan, tilted his hat and grinned at his son. "I guess I'd better take a look at that critter."

Danny beamed with excitement, a grin that faded as the dull roar of a vehicle engine caught his father's attention.

A rusted pickup truck was bouncing along the edge of the alfalfa field. Shading her eyes, Susan recognized the truck as belonging to Samuel. She watched as it parked beside Jarod's much newer and larger vehicle. A moment later, a familiar, bowlegged figure stepped out, dusted a worn hat on his thighs, then settled the headgear with a subtle yank that sent a shiver down Susan's spine.

Something was wrong. She could feel it.

Behind her, Danny issued a plaintive wail. "Come on, Dad, come look. Please?"

"In a minute, son." Jarod was already moving toward Samuel.

Susan suspected it would take considerably longer than a minute for him to complete whatever business the ranch foreman had to discuss. Judging by Danny's disheartened expression, the child knew that, too. Her heart went out to the dejected youngster.

Pasting on a bright smile, she picked her way across the rocky ground. "I've never seen a catfish, sweetie. Would it be too much trouble for you to point it out to me?"

The boy's smile wasn't nearly as bright as it had been for his father. But it was bright enough to warm Susan's heart.

Samuel paused about halfway between the pond and the edge of the field where both pickup trucks were parked. The older man shifted, spat on the ground and was watching the chugging harvesting machine when Jarod caught up with him.

"Them's sloppy bales." Samuel nodded toward the massive alfalfa rolls dotting the harvested portion of the field. "Best have maintenance do a look-see. Baling belts probably shook loose."

Jarod glanced over, gave an affirmative nod. "Tell Mick to fill out a maintenance requisition after the east and west fields have been mowed."

"Yup." Samuel spat again and glanced past Jarod's shoulder, back toward the cow pond. "Y'all have a nice picnic?"

"Hmm?" Jarod blinked, saw the remnants of their lunch still stacked neatly on the tail gate of his truck. "Yes, it was terrific. Fried chicken, baked beans, potato salad. A real feast."

"Family is a good thing. A man needs his family." Folding his wiry arms, Samuel frowned, puckered his mouth until it wrinkled in on itself, and seemed to disappear into a jaw dotted with gray stubble.

Jarod regarded his old friend, recognized a thin veil of worry in his eyes. "Did the boys get the market steers moved into the trucking pasture?"

"Yup, sure did. Got 'em checking the grazing line now. They'll be ready to truck in a week or so." Samuel scratched his chin, continued to stare at the harvester as if fascinated by each puff of diesel smoke belching from the exhaust stack. "So, how's the missus been feeling lately? She and the little one doing right well, are they?"

"Couldn't be better." Brightening, Jarod reached into his shirt pocket, proudly handed his friend the ultrasound photograph taken two days earlier. "That's my daughter. Isn't she beautiful?"

Samuel blinked. "Compared to what?"

Frowning, Jarod glanced at the photo. "You're holding it upside down."

"How can you tell?"

"Because that—" he pointed to a lovely round shadow "—is her head...see? This is an arm...look you can even see the little fingers...and these are her knees."

"Oh."

"Ultrasound pictures aren't exactly like a regular snapshot."

Samuel looked down at the cloudy image. "That's for sure."

"But if you really look closely, you can see her little nose, and—"

Susan's amused voice cut him off. "Good grief, Jarod, give the poor man a break." Grinning, Susan walked toward them, her arm tossed around Danny, who hobbled beside her with his cane. "To anyone except a doting parent, that photograph resembles nothing more than a nondescript white cloud floating in a cone of smoke."

Relieved, Samuel pressed the photo back in Jarod's hand. "Yup, yup, that's just what it looks like. A right pretty white cloud, though, right pretty indeed."

Susan chuckled. "Don't feel bad, Samuel. Jarod even showed it to the checker at the grocery store and wouldn't pay the bill until she agreed it was the prettiest in-utero infant she'd ever seen in her life."

Stung, Jarod glanced down at the precious photo. "It's not that nondescript, and the checker really did seem to be impressed by how pretty Elisa Jane is."

"You mean Tiffany Dior."

Jarod snorted. "Sounds like a jewelry store."

"Better than sounding like someone's maiden aunt."

"Elisa Jane is a beautiful and simple name."

"Tiffany Dior has class."

"It's pretentious."

"It's poetic."

"It's—"

Danny tugged Jarod's sleeve and blurted, "Show Samuel my picture, Dad, the one of me in my baseball uniform."

"I'm sure Samuel has seen that one, son."

"Show him again! You still have it, don't you, Dad? I mean, you said you'd never take it out of your wallet. You didn't, did you?"

"Of course I didn't." Smiling, Jarod slipped the ultrasound photograph back into his pocket. "I wouldn't go anywhere without my favorite picture of my favorite boy, would I?"

Relief flooded the youngster's eyes. He shook his head, but his smile seemed a bit thin. Susan stepped over, slipped her arm around the boy's shoulder. There was a peculiar expression on her face, but her gaze flickered to Samuel before Jarod had the chance to consider what it might mean.

"How's Martha's sister, Samuel?" Susan asked.

The older man swallowed hard. "Not good, not good at all."

"I'm so sorry. Martha must be terribly upset. I know how close she and her sister are."

"Yup, and that's a fact." Samuel lifted his hat, wiped his brow with his forearm. "Marty's right upset."

Confused, Jarod finally spoke up. "I didn't realize Martha's sister was ill." Truthfully, he hadn't even known that Martha had a sister, and was chagrined to realize that Susan seemed to know more about the woman who had been his friend and employee for nearly a decade than he did himself. "What's wrong with her?"

Samuel sighed, glanced away. Susan laid a comforting hand on his shoulder, then turned toward Jarod. "Martha's sister was diagnosed with pancreatic cancer about two months ago."

"Two months—" Jarod's voice gave out. He swallowed hard, shook his head, cleared his throat. "God, I'm so sorry. Why didn't anyone tell me?"

Samuel answered. "Marty doesn't like to spread family business around. Y'all had enough to worry about. Thing is, the doctors say Ethel don't have much time. Marty kinda wants to be with her when the good Lord calls."

"Of course," Jarod murmured. He felt like he'd been kicked in the gut. How could he have not known what someone so dear to him had been going through? Had he been that wrapped up with his own life, his own problems, that his closest friends felt they couldn't share their troubles with him?

"You tell Martha to go," Susan said firmly. "Tell her not to worry about a thing. I'm not half the cook she is, and I'm a lousy housekeeper to boot, but I can still keep the place running until she gets back."

Samuel didn't look convinced. "She don't want to be leaving you alone, what with the young'un due so soon."

"Nonsense. The baby isn't due for several weeks." Susan shot a questioning glance at Jarod, who seemed to be still in shock. "I may be speaking out of turn here, but if you and Martha need a little extra cash to help with travel expenses, I'm sure we can work something out."

At that point, Jarod managed to shake himself into a reasonably coherent state. "I'll have my travel agent make all the arrangements. Don't worry about cost. We'll take care of it."

"No, no, that ain't right." Samuel shook his head, his eyes a bit too moist, too bright. "We ain't paupers."

"You and Martha are my dearest friends," Jarod said. "This is nothing compared to all you've given to me and mine over the years. Please, let me do this for you."

Samuel wouldn't meet his eyes. He sniffed, nodded, wiped his face before tugging on his hat. "The market herd will be reading for loading next week," he murmured.

Then he spun on his heel, returned to his truck and drove away.

"Why didn't you tell me about Martha's sister?"

The pain in Jarod's eyes touched Susan. She shifted on the truck's bench seat, bracing herself on the dashboard as he turned into the long, winding driveway that led to the ranch house. "I didn't know myself until a few days ago."

Susan had been home all day since summer school had ended, so Martha had asked for, and received, a cutback in her housekeeping duties. Since Jarod had been concerned about Susan performing heavy housework, Martha had agreed to come twice weekly. Susan hadn't argued the point, not because she felt incapable of washing windows or cleaning woodwork, but because she truly enjoyed Martha's company and looked forward to her visits.

"Martha mentioned last week that her sister's health was failing." It had been one of the first personal statements Martha had made, and a breakthrough of sorts in their relationship. "She needed someone to talk to about her pain, and her fear. I listened. We hugged, cried, and she asked me not to tell anyone."

Jarod issued a snort that made Danny glance up from his appointed spot between the two adults.

"I'm not just anyone," Jarod snapped. "You should have told me."

"I won't betray a friend's confidence." Susan skimmed a worried glance over Danny's head. "I'm sorry if you're angry with me."

The truck stopped so quickly she barely had time to brace herself. Jarod shifted into Park, pivoted in his seat. His eyes were wide, disbelieving. Stunned. "Angry with you? My God, I could never be angry with you."

When Susan felt the air slip out of her lungs all at once, she realized she'd been holding her breath. "I'm glad," she whispered. "It would hurt me terribly if you were."

His eyes softened, his lips loosened. He reached around his son to caress the side of Susan's face. "I'd never hurt you. Never."

Susan's heart swelled with a joy she'd never experienced before. "I know."

The simplicity of that statement took her breath away, because it was true. For the first time in her life, she felt emotionally safe, secure in the knowledge that this special and unique man would never turn his back on her, never betray her, never abandon her or their precious child.

An electric tension swelled up inside the cramped cab, a crackle of passion so intense that her scalp prickled with it. They shared the same bed, had since that exquisite night of lovemaking so many weeks ago. But they hadn't made love since their last clinic visit, when the doctor had suggested that it might be prudent to cut back on sexual relations until after the baby was born.

Jarod had accepted the edict instantly. Susan, however, had been surprised and frightened. Despite the doctor's reassurance that it was merely a precaution due to the infant's position low in the womb, Susan was still nervous, and had been even more careful in her daily activities.

But she did so miss the passion, the heat of their lovemaking. Missed it more than she dared admit, even to herself.

Between them, Danny squirmed. "Geez, are you guys gonna sit there all day? My leg is cramping and stuff."

Jarod blinked, smiled, shoved the truck into gear. "Sorry, son. I was just mesmerized by incredible beauty."

Danny folded his arms, and stared out the front window, while Susan blushed, and giggled like a schoolgirl. Before she'd met Jarod Bodine, it had never occurred to her that so much happiness was even possible. Now it didn't occur to her that it could ever end.

Until they pulled up in front of the house, and her heart sank like a stone.

She didn't recognize the sedate gray sedan parked in the driveway. She did, however, recognize the somber-faced lawyer hovering on the front porch, a stark reminder of just how tenuous that happiness was.

The photograph taunted Jarod. He stared at it, vaguely aware of the droning voice from the guest chair behind him. The picture was of his father and his grandfather and himself. Bodine men.

Chapter Eleven

The photograph taunted Jarod. He stared at it, vaguely aware of the droning voice from the guest chair behind him. The picture was of his father and his grandfather and himself. Bodine men.

The wall was filled with photographs, a legacy of the land and the family that had carved a life here. There were snapshots of the ranch's history, a smiling group of men showing off a newly built barn, Grandpa Bodine with his first champion bull, Vernon Bodine, Jarod's father, with his favorite horse, and a prized picture of three generations of Bodine men taken when Jarod was about seven.

No photographs of Bodine women graced the office wall. Jarod wondered why he'd never noticed that lapse before. Sky View Ranch had been built by sweat, by blood, by desperation and determination. But it had not been built by men alone.

It was Jarod's grandmother who had negotiated the land purchase that doubled the size of the ranch, providing enough grazing acreage to sustain a profitable herd. It was Jarod's own mother who had created the maintenance yard, the machine shop, the barracks areas to house the temporary personnel necessary for the peak labor periods of calving and shipping seasons. It was Gail who had created an island of culture and beauty in the midst of a dusty, calloused plain.

And it was Susan—beautiful, precious Susan—who had brought the miracle of love and understanding into the lives of an angry, frightened little boy and his grieving, guilt-scarred father.

So now Jarod studied the photographs of tribute, of victory and validation. He studied them and he wondered...where were the women?

Behind him, attorney Davis Grayson's voice droned on, a one-sided discussion of legal liabilities and contractual obligations, of land-use proposals and the litigation potential of the petition drive to which he'd lent both his name and his support. Legal stuff, lawyer talk, all vital, all necessary, all boring as hell.

All preludes to the true purpose of the attorney's visit. A purpose that chilled Jarod to the marrow.

A door hinge creaked, instantly garnering Jarod's attention. He spun on his heel as Susan entered the room.

She issued a nervous smile, softly closed the door behind her. "I fixed Danny a snack. He's in his room playing a computer game."

Davis, who'd stood as she entered, pulled one of the armchairs out for her.

She murmured her thanks, grasped the chair arms and lowered herself slowly. "I feel like a blimp."

"You're beautiful." Jarod spoke so quickly, with such emphasis that Susan widened her eyes and his attorney raised a brow.

"Pregnancy does agree with you," Davis added kindly. "You are positively radiant."

She eyed them both with blatant suspicion. "My, if I didn't know better, I'd suspect you both were trying to butter me up to sign something."

Davis flushed, seated himself. "Merely finalizing a few formalities." He placed his briefcase on his lap, flipped it open to extract several legal documents. "As we discussed some months ago, there are some loose ends to tie up before the child is delivered. I've taken the liberties of preparing a draft document for your perusal."

He handed one to Susan, one to Jarod, kept the third for his own reference.

Jarod laid his copy on the desk without a glance. His attention was riveted on Susan. She scanned the first page, then the second, paling slightly although her stoic expression didn't waver.

Davis cleared his throat. "As you'll see, Mrs. Bodine, arrangements have been made to secure adequate living quarters for you and the child immediately after the delivery. I think you'll agree that my client has been quite generous in our offer of support—"

Susan interrupted. "Perhaps I am mistaken, Mr. Grayson, but I was under the impression that you were retained to protect the rights of the baby, not of either of the parents."

The lawyer blinked. "Technically, that's quite true. However—"

"In that case, I'd respectfully request that these documents be rewritten to reflect that in matters pertaining to her custody and future rights, our unborn daughter is your client.''

Bewildered, Davis glanced toward Jarod for assistance, and received only a smile and a shrug.

''Yes,'' he murmured, frowning at the documents. He snatched a pen from his breast pocket, scribbled a few marginal notes. ''Continuing to summarize, my cli—er, Mr. Bodine's only demands are the liberal visitation, as specified in appendix A, and further delineated in sub-addendums I, IV, and X, and your agreement to reside a proximity of no more than sixty miles from Mr. Bodine's dwelling until the child—''

''Your client.'' Susan smiled sweetly.

''Ah, yes, until my client reaches the age of majority.''

She nodded. ''Unfortunately, I cannot agree to the proximity clause. As currently written, it would preclude our daughter from going away to college, visiting friends and relatives outside the specified parameters, or making her own decisions about living arrangements even after she'd reached an age where she would be entitled to have a say in such matters.''

''Well, I assure you that such strict interpretation would never be enforced by my cl—by Mr. Bodine.''

''But as our daughter's attorney, we expect you to look after her best interests, and her best interests are not served by legal clauses that limit her options.'' Susan glanced at Jarod with a wide-eyed innocence that didn't fool him for a minute. ''Would you not agree, Mr. Bodine?''

God, she was magnificent. Jarod beamed with pride. ''I would absolutely agree, Mrs. Bodine.''

The perplexed lawyer glanced from Jarod to Susan and back again. He swallowed, frowned, removed his wire-framed glasses and tucked them into the breast pocket of his suit coat. "I seem to be at a disadvantage here. It was my understanding that Mrs. Bodine wished to move into private living quarters with the infant as soon as possible after the birth, at which time the dissolution of marriage papers, which you both have previously agreed upon, would be officially filed with the court. Has your position on that matter changed?"

When Susan glanced away without comment, Davis turned his attention to Jarod and questioned him with a look.

Jarod shuffled, folded his arms and propped a hip against the corner of his desk. "There really isn't any rush, is there, Susan? I mean, you're free to leave as we'd originally planned, of course. But that doesn't mean you *have* to leave."

Her gaze shifted, met his. He saw a spark of hope in her eyes. "Of course, there's no rush at all. I mean, beyond the inconvenience of having two more people in the house—"

"That is not an inconvenience." Jarod's interruption was delivered so forcefully that the attorney's head snapped around. Jarod coughed, issued a thin smile, tried for a more leisurely tone. "You are welcome to stay here as long as you're comfortable."

Susan regarded him. "Is that what you want, Jarod?"

He spoke quickly, without considering that she might be seeking some reassurance. "It's what you want that counts."

Her smile trembled at the edges. "Perhaps you've forgotten the trauma and sleepless nights that go along with newborns."

"There's no greater joy." Jarod meant that, although thoughts of his daughter's birth evoked mixed feelings, the miracle of a precious new life followed by the despair of inevitable loss. He addressed the attorney. "Perhaps...we could just play it by ear, see how things go. I mean, if that's all right with Susan."

"It is." The words were out of her mouth before Jarod had finished his sentence. She flushed slightly. "That is, I realize that eventually Tiffany Dior—"

"Elisa Jane." Jarod smiled.

Susan smiled back. "Our daughter and I will have to find a place of our own." She paused a beat, her smile fading. "That was the agreement...wasn't it?"

Jarod's own smile hardened at the edges. "Yes, that was the agreement."

Moistening her lips, Susan's gaze edged away. "But I don't suppose there's any urgency to the move."

"No," Jarod agreed. "No urgency at all."

"And it might be best for the baby—"

"Definitely best for the baby."

"Extra time here would give Danny the opportunity to bond with his sister."

Jarod nodded so hard his hat slipped. "Sibling bonds are important."

The attorney, who'd been watching the exchange with obvious astonishment, leaned back in his chair. "Am I to assume that you'd prefer to contact me at a later time in regards to these, er, arrangements?"

Susan and Jarod blurted, "Yes!" at the same moment. They laughed nervously, both shifted in place.

"We'll call you," Jarod told Davis. "Later."

Frowning, Davis gathered the draft documents, replaced them in his briefcase. He stood, hesitated. "I must counsel you both that agreement on matters of this importance are best determined in advance. It truly is in the best interest of the child that an amicable and legally binding determination be made as soon as possible. After the child is born, emotions may overwhelm rational thought and—''

''I said we'll call you.'' Pushing away from his relaxed pose beside the desk, Jarod straightened, tensed, and spoke through clenched teeth. ''Thank you for your time, Davis. We'll be in touch.''

Dismissed and clearly deflated, the lawyer sighed, nodded, gathered his possessions and strode out the door.

A nervous silence filled the room. Susan fiddled with a thread on the sleeve of her maternity smock. Jarod made a production of gathering loose paper clips from his desk top, and tucking them into a magnetic container.

''Well,'' Susan said finally. She licked her lips, appeared inordinately interested in the condition of her fingernails. ''I'd better start supper.''

''If you're tired, I can fix something.''

''I'm not tired.''

Jarod wasn't convinced. She looked exhausted. He feared that today's outing had been too much for her. ''Thing is, I'm in the mood for meatloaf, and nobody makes a meatloaf I like except me.''

She glanced up, eyes wide. ''You like Martha's meatloaf.''

''That's because I taught her how to make it.''

''Fine. You taught her, you can teach me.''

''No, I can't. The recipe is a family secret.''

''How secret can it be if you've already given it to Martha?''

''She beat it out of me.''

"Which is what I'm about to do."

Jarod taunted her with a grin. "Under the circumstances, I'm pretty sure I can outrun you."

She shot him a squinty-eyed stare. "Sleep lightly, Mr. Bodine, lest you awaken to find a sensitive portion of your anatomy glued to your navel."

The wry comment evoked a bark of laughter. Her humor was sharp, dry and frequently unexpected. He loved it. "At least let me help you fix dinner. We'll do it together."

Her gaze softened. "I'd like that."

"So would I," Jarod murmured. "So would I."

A swirl of dark clouds hugged the horizon. An early autumn storm was brewing to the west. It would cover the ranch by nightfall, Susan thought. The autumn air was brisk, chillier than it had been only a few hours earlier.

She gathered a small bag of cut carrots, and headed toward the stable, only to pause on the pathway as she saw Danny bouncing a basketball behind the old barn. Judging by his brooding expression, he was still in a foul mood, and had been since Martha had left to visit her ill sister.

Susan was worried about him, about the emotional distance that had crept into his demeanor over the past week. She pasted on a cheery smile, and walked toward him. "Hi, sweetie. What are you doing?"

Danny glanced up, rolled his eyes. "What does it look like?"

"It looks like you're bouncing a basketball."

"Duh." Scowling, the boy turned his back to her. Susan glanced around, saw his cane propped against the barn wall. "I take it your leg is feeling better to-day?"

He bounced the ball without reply.

Susan shifted, chewed her lip for a moment. "I was going up to the stable to give the horses some carrots. You know how Buttermilk thrives on the attention." The child gave no indication of having heard her. "Would you like to join me? Elton says the horses miss your visits."

Although Danny didn't respond, Susan saw a light tremor slip along his shoulders. He stopped bouncing the ball, hugged it to his chest without turning to face her.

"You had another bad dream last night, didn't you?" She paused, in case he chose to answer. He didn't. "Your dad said you wouldn't tell him what the dream was about." She paused again. "You know what I think?" Silence. "I think it was about Thunder. I think you miss Thunder and would really like to go see him to make sure he's all right."

The boy's entire body shuddered. "You don't know anything."

"Then why don't you tell me where I'm wrong?"

To Susan's shock, Danny spun around. His face was red, contorted. His eyes bright with tears. "Why should I? You're the teacher. You're supposed to know everything, but you don't. You don't know *anything!*"

Flinging the ball aside, Danny threw himself forward and half ran, half hobbled around the side of the barn.

Stunned, Susan stood there for several minutes. Then she retrieved the child's cane and dragged her tired body up the path to the stables.

* * *

"The laundry hamper is empty."

Jarod glanced up from the chaos of painted parts and fastening hardware strewn across the living-room floor. "That's a good thing, isn't it?"

She planted her hands somewhere behind the sides of her stomach, gave him a narrowed stare. "Last night it was overflowing with dirty laundry. Now it is empty and the dresser drawers are filled with clean, folded clothing."

"A real disaster," Jarod murmured. Seated cross-legged on the floor, he flinched, straightened out one cramping leg. "I can see why you'd be distressed."

The tweak of a smile tugged Susan's lush lips. "I doubt the laundry fairy magically appeared while we were in church this morning, so that leads me to the only logical conclusion."

He frowned at the assembly instructions, bewildered by the complexity. It was embarrassing that a man capable of welding a squeeze chute out of scrap steel couldn't figure out how to put a simple bassinet together. "What conclusion is that?"

"The conclusion that you spent the night washing clothes instead of getting the rest you need."

"It's Sunday. Other than performing a few stable chores and a routine check of the herds, I've got the day off. Say, you didn't see a Phillips screwdriver around here, did you?" He looked under a colorful plastic bumper pad, shoved a stack of jig-sawed wooden parts aside. "Assembling a space shuttle would be easier."

Claude ambled over, purring helpfully. He rubbed his head on Jarod's shoulder, then climbed into his lap and seated himself in front of the assembly diagram Jarod was attempting to decipher.

"Claude, you aren't helping." Jarod shifted the animal aside, shook out the rumpled instruction sheet, compared it to the assembly instructions and saw no discernable correlation between the two. "What the devil is a cradle foot? And why does it need to be affixed to a headboard baluster? And what the devil is a headboard baluster in the first place?"

Issuing a pained sigh, Susan sighed, crossed the room and glanced over his shoulder. "It's upside down."

"The headboard baluster is upside down?"

"The blueprint thingy." She plucked the diagram from his hand, turned it and placed it back into his palms. "Seriously, Jarod, you needn't coddle me so. I'm quite capable of stuffing garments into a machine and turning the knob."

"Of course you are." He glanced up, saw the fatigue in her eyes and felt as if his heart had been squeezed. When she laid a hand on his shoulder, he instinctively turned to kiss each knuckle. "I'm just particular about my clothes, that's all."

She chuckled under her breath. "This from a man who has been known to wear his shirts inside out."

It was a truth Jarod didn't bother to dispute. He'd never much cared what kind of clothing covered his body as long as it kept the sage from scratching him bloody. Susan knew that about him. She knew a great deal about him.

And he knew a great deal about her as well.

Although Susan never complained, Jarod had noticed her stamina waning as the pregnancy took a physical toll. She was pale all the time now, and he'd seen her flinching, rubbing the small of her back when she thought he wasn't looking. "I don't mind doing laundry."

"You hate doing laundry."

She was right, of course. He did hate it. "What I really hate is anything that arrives in pieces, with the words *some assembly required* on the box."

Susan smiled, took two steps and plucked a Phillips screwdriver from a nearby end table. Jarod accepted the item with an embarrassed mutter, turned his attention back to the task at hand.

"Aha!" Jarod located a flat, painted piece that looked suspiciously like the drawing of the headboard baluster. "By jove, I think I've got this sucker figured out—"

The front door burst open. "Dad, Dad, there are a whole bunch of geese flying right above us. They're in a really neat V formation and they're honking and everything."

Jarod shuffled through a pile of screws, mumbled without looking up. "That's nice."

"Come out and see them, Dad!"

"Not right now, son. I'm trying to assemble this bassinet for your baby sister."

"Oh."

From the corner of his eye Jarod saw Susan move toward the front door.

"I'd like to see the geese, Danny." She reached out to ruffle his hair, as was her habit. "Let's go outside, and you can show them to me."

The boy turned away, shoved his hands into the pockets of his thick denim jacket. "They're just a bunch of dumb birds."

Susan pulled her hand back, clasped her fingers together. "Would you like some hot chocolate and a sandwich?"

"I'm not hungry." Danny crossed the room, scooped Claude into his arms. "Tomorrow's the first day of school, Dad."

"I know." Jarod glanced up, smiling. "You must be pretty darned excited. It's been a long time since you've seen some of your friends."

"Yeah." Danny grinned, shifted the fat cat to his shoulder as if it were a human infant. "Susan said maybe you'd take me, on account of it being the first day and all."

Jarod froze for a moment, then slipped a glance at Susan and saw the final trace of color slip from her cheeks. "Susan?"

"Yeah. You know…her." Danny nodded in Susan's general direction.

It was the first time Jarod had heard Danny refer to Susan by her first name. Before the wedding he'd called her Miss Mitchell; afterward he'd called her Mom. Jarod didn't know quite what to make of this new, rather disrespectful manner of speech. "Please don't refer to Susan as 'her,' Danny. It's impolite."

Susan cleared her throat. "It's all right, Jarod."

"No, it's not all right." Laying down the screwdriver, Jarod propped his elbows on his thighs and watched his son's expression turn ominous.

Still wringing her hands, Susan stepped forward with a bright, tense smile. "Jarod, I'll bet Danny could help you with your project. If you worked together, you'd probably be done soon enough to play basketball before supper."

Danny responded without looking at her. Instead,

he skewered Jarod with a harsh stare. "Can't play basketball without a hoop."

The reminder that he'd promised to install a basketball hoop weeks ago cut like a knife. "You're right, son. After you were hurt, I pretty much forgot about it. Now that you're nearly back to speed, we'll give that a top priority."

Danny's gaze slipped to the scatter of enameled wooden pieces stenciled with bright balloons and baby animals. "Yeah, right."

A desperate cheeriness crept into Susan's voice. "You know, there's no rush about assembling the bassinet. Why don't you and Danny spend the afternoon installing his basketball hoop instead."

"The baby is due in a few more weeks," Jarod said. "At the rate I'm going, that may not be long enough."

She issued an edgy chuckle. "I have more faith in you than that." She plucked the instruction sheet from his hand. "Besides, it's much too nice a day to be stuck inside."

Jarod studied the panic in her eyes, and wondered where it had come from. "It's forty degrees outside."

"Only if you factor in the wind chill. Hey, the sun is shining and the sky is blue! An outdoorsy type like yourself should be thrilled for the opportunity to breathe nice, crisp autumn air."

He blinked at the ludicrous suggestion that a man who spent ninety percent of his life working outdoors was fresh-air-deprived. "You're right. I'm never outside. What was I thinking?"

Susan exhaled all at once, skewered him with a look. "For heaven's sake, will you please put up your son's basketball hoop?"

Before Jarod could reply, Danny pushed the cat off

his shoulder. "Who cares about a dumb hoop? I don't even want one. I don't want to go fishing, either. I hate fishing. I hate basketball."

"Now wait a minute, son." Jarod stood, reached out as the boy ducked under his hand.

"I'm glad you're not going to drive me to school. I never wanted you to." Sniffing, Danny wiped his eyes, sidestepped toward the hall. "I hate school. It's dumb. School is dumb and basketball is dumb and fishing is dumb."

With that the boy pivoted around and ran down the hall. A moment later, his bedroom door slammed, and Claude dived behind the living-room sofa.

Jarod was stunned. "What in hell was that all about?"

A sweet scent wafted around him. "Give him a couple of minutes," Susan whispered. "Then go talk to him. He needs his daddy."

"I don't understand." He slipped his arm around Susan, brushed a slip of blond hair from her face. "Why is he so angry?"

"He's frightened, I think. The first day of school, when he's been away for so long. It's unnerving. And you've been so busy, I think he feels a little…ignored."

The gentle edge she placed on that final word got his attention. "Do you think Danny is jealous of the baby?"

"I think he feels as if some of the attention that was rightfully his has been diverted." Susan lowered her gaze, but not before Jarod saw the worry in her eyes. "Danny has been through a stressful time, an arduous recovery from a painful injury, and the sudden appearance of someone else in his father's life."

Jarod slipped a thumb under her chin, urging her to look at him. "Danny adores you."

"He adores you more," she whispered. "And he should. You are his father."

"I don't understand. This isn't a game. Nobody is keeping score."

"Danny is." Susan stepped from his embrace reluctantly. She looked so fragile, so very tired. It was all Jarod could do to keep from gathering her in his arms, and protecting her from the entire world. "I don't know what Danny is thinking, because he chooses not to communicate with me."

She flinched, and for the first time Jarod realized how hurt she was by Danny's rejection.

"I do know," she said quietly, "that from Danny's perspective it must seem as if you are more concerned about me and the baby than you are about him."

"That's not true." Even as the words still reverberated in the air, Jarod wondered if they were spoken with too much force to be believed. "Of course I'm concerned about you and the baby. That doesn't mean I love my son any less."

"I know that, and you know that. We need to make certain that Danny knows that, too." She turned, issued a smile that trembled just slightly. "Danny needs more of your time, more of your attention."

Despite the ring of truth her words evoked, Jarod was suddenly tense, annoyed at a reality he didn't quite recognize and chose not to explore. "Danny has to realize that he's not the center of the universe. Other people matter, too."

"Jarod!"

"Don't give me that shocked look, Susan. We both

know he's spoiled, and we both know that's my fault, not his."

"He's a child, a little boy. It's normal for him to be consumed by his own thoughts, his own feelings. Right now he's a frightened little boy, afraid the daddy who is his whole life is turning away from him."

"I'm not turning away from him, dammit. I'm just not jumping every time he barks an order."

Susan stared as if seeing him for the first time. "There is more than one way for a father to abandon his child."

Only after she'd left the room did Jarod understand the enormity of what he had done.

Chapter Twelve

Susan spread the covers over Danny's bed, tucked in the corners of the bedclothes and straightened, rubbing the cramp in her lower back. She glanced around the mussed room, knowing that the boy was supposed to keep it tidy himself. Still, she couldn't prevent herself from gathering the pile of soiled garments beside his computer table, and tucking a few errant toys on the closet shelf. Jarod would disapprove, she supposed. He'd been much stricter with the boy over the past few weeks, which had resulted in Danny becoming even more sullen and belligerent.

She blamed herself for that.

The sound of Jarod's voice startled her. She spun around, her guilty gaze darting around the empty room. A moment later he spoke again, and she realized that he was on the telephone in his office, which shared a wall with Danny's bedroom. Relieved, she shifted the laundry in her arms and left the child's room.

As she moved down the hallway, a glint of morning sunlight sprayed from the open door to the guest room. She peered inside, and saw Danny staring at the bassinet that had taken his father the better half of a Sunday afternoon to construct.

While Susan watched, the boy reached inside the bassinet to retrieve a small stuffed cow that Jarod had brought home last week. A gift for the baby, he'd explained, a symbol of her heritage. Susan had been ridiculously pleased by the gesture.

She cleared her throat. "It's adorable, isn't it? Do you think your sister will like it?"

Danny spun around as if shot, flung the stuffed animal back into the bassinet. The softness that had glazed his gaze moments ago now hardened into open defiance. "Who cares? It's just a dumb toy."

Susan tensed, chose her words cautiously. Over the past weeks she had laboriously attempted to include Danny in the birth process, to little avail. She tried yet again. "What kind of toys do you think she might prefer?"

"I dunno." He shrugged. "Babies are stupid anyway."

On cue, a potent little limb flailed inside her womb. Susan grunted, grasped her belly. "Oh my. I don't think she liked being called stupid."

Danny paled. He chewed his lip, took a tentative step forward. "What's she doing?"

"Just a friendly kick to let me know who's boss— Oh!" Stumbling forward, Susan dropped the laundry on the guest bed and perched on the edge of the mattress. "My, she is frisky this morning."

Danny hesitated, took another step forward and eyed her stomach warily. At that moment the baby rotated, causing a visible bulge beneath the stretched cotton T-shirt Susan wore. Danny's eyes popped. "Wow, I could see that."

Sensing an opportunity, Susan reached out. "Give me your hand."

Without hesitation, the boy did so, and allowed Susan to place his small palm over the most active area. In seconds, they were rewarded by movement.

Danny's eyes widened, his lips parted in awe. "Geez, she's really strong."

"Yes, she certainly is."

"Do you think she can, you know, hear us and stuff?"

"Studies indicate that babies can indeed hear voices and other sound stimulus from outside the womb."

"So she can hear me talking?"

"I would imagine so."

The thought seemed to pain him. "Do you think she knows I'm her brother?"

Susan smiled. "I'm sure she does."

After digesting that for a moment, Danny's lips again tightened and he yanked his hand away. "Babies are lame," he announced. "All they do is poop and cry and stuff. I wish she'd just go away."

Susan saw the conflict in Danny's eyes, sensed his turmoil in being both fascinated with his unborn sibling and simultaneously threatened by her. "You may feel differently later," she said evenly. "You're not as angry with Thunder as you were several months ago, are you? I saw the lovely portrait you drew of him standing tall and proud in the pasture."

The child's lip quivered, his eyes brightened with

moisture. "I hate horses. Horses are dumb and mean, and I wish they'd all die."

"I don't think that's true, sweetie."

"It is true!" Danny shouted. "I hate horses and I hate babies and I hate you."

Before Susan could react, the child was jerked backward, spun around to face his furious father. Susan hadn't even seen Jarod enter the room. Now he grasped his son's arm with more rage in his eyes than she had ever seen him display. "Don't you ever, I mean *ever,* speak to your stepmother like that again."

Tears spurted down the boy's cheeks. "She's not my stepmother, not really. So I do hate her, I do, I do, I do—"

The slap reverberated through the room like a gunshot. Susan gasped in horror, covered her mouth. Jarod had never raised a hand to his son before. She was stunned, sickened, twisted by guilt at having caused this terrible rift between father and son.

The anger drained from Jarod's eyes instantly. He released his grasp on the sobbing boy's arm, raked his own hair in frustration. "I'm sorry, son. I shouldn't have done that—"

"I hate you, too!" Danny screamed, pressing his palm against his red cheek. "I hate everybody in the whole world!"

With that furious pronouncement, the child dashed to his bedroom and slammed the door.

Winding her arms around her belly, Susan curled protectively forward. She was sick inside and felt the sting of Danny's pain as acutely as if she was the one who'd been slapped. "My God, Jarod."

Clearly distressed, he pinched the bridge of his nose, struggling to compose himself. "I had no right to do that, I know. But I can't allow him to treat you with such disrespect, even if he didn't really mean it.''

Miserably, Susan looked up. ''Don't you see, Jarod? He did mean it.'' She moistened her lips, shook her head, and fought her own surging tears.

Susan understood all too well what Danny was feeling, the rage, the helplessness, the fear. There was only one way to help a grieving child cope with that terrifying tangle of emotion.

It broke Susan's heart.

Entering the house slowly, Susan felt like a lumbering rhinoceros. The walk to the stables became more grueling every day. Today had been particularly difficult, with a bone-chilling wind blowing in from the northwest and the promise of snow in the air. Her back was killing her, her ankles were swollen to nearly twice their normal size, and sharp pains shooting down her inner thighs were searing enough to make her gasp.

The blare of television cartoons greeted her. Danny was sprawled on the floor, watching some kind of superhero save a city she'd never heard of. She shrugged out of her heavy wool jacket, laid the empty carrot bag on the entry table. ''The stable hand says Buttermilk won't leave her stall for exercise today.'' Buttermilk was touted as the equine equivalent of a weather psychic. ''I guess those black clouds hanging over the mesa must mean a real storm is brewing.''

Danny didn't so much as favor her with a glance.

Sighing, Susan lowered herself into a lounge chair, kicked off her sneakers, which remained unlaced since her feet were nearly as swollen as her ankles. She'd have killed for a good foot rub. Unfortunately she hadn't even seen her feet in weeks, let alone reached them. Only the throbbing at the ends of her legs reminded her that the toe-studded appendages were still there.

Claude leaped softly into her lap with a supportive trill. Susan stroked the animal, smiling when he pressed his head against her chin. "You are a sweet boy," she murmured to the cat. "Even if you do leave grasshoppers the size of Kansas on my bed."

Claude meowed and promptly began to knead her lap with his sharp kitty claws. Susan flinched, deflected the affectionate wounding until the satisfied cat curled into a comfortable nap position and went to sleep.

Shifting her attention, she regarded Danny for a moment, studied the boy as he stared mesmerized at the TV screen. "Have you finished your Saturday chores yet?" She paused a beat, then two, then gave him a full minute to respond. He didn't. "You know your father will probably be here in an hour or so. It's the first question he's going to ask."

Again the boy gave no indication that he'd heard her.

Susan's heart felt as if it had been scraped raw. She had done the unthinkable, had become a wedge between a truly good father and the son he adored. "Danny, sweetie, you must know that your dad loves you more than anything in this world."

The comment evoked a lowering of the child's gaze, a tremor in his small shoulder. But he said nothing.

"Danny—" The distant roar of a truck engine cut her off. She sighed. "Your dad is home."

Danny fidgeted, kept his eyes glued to the television screen.

A moment later, Jarod tromped into the room, pulling off his leather gloves. "Nippy out there."

"Buttermilk thinks a storm is coming," Susan replied.

"Buttermilk is right." Jarod stuffed the gloves into his jacket pocket, angled a sheepish glance. "I forgot, uh, some wire clippers."

Susan smiled. Every day for the past two weeks Jarod had shown up around noon, having forgotten one tool or another. She knew perfectly well that he was much too organized to have forgotten anything. As her pregnancy had progressed, he'd become more and more solicitous, more and more concerned. Appearing once, sometimes twice throughout the day was his method of assuring himself that she was all right.

No one had every truly worried about Susan before. Well, no one beyond her two sisters, who lived too far away to offer her more than telephoned moral support. Rather than being annoyed by Jarod's tendency to hover around her, she actually appreciated it, was touched by his concern.

"I haven't seen any wire cutters here in the house," she said.

He glanced away, hung his hat on a wall peg and shrugged out of his jacket. "I thought I'd go ahead and fix myself a sandwich as long as I was here."

Susan started to rise. "I'll fix it."

"No." He crossed the room, laid a warm palm on her shoulder. "I can do it. You rest." He glanced at Danny, who was still sprawled across the floor. "Have you finished your Saturday chores?"

The child scratched his rib cage. "Almost."

"Almost isn't good enough," Jarod said kindly.

"The rule is no television or computer games before chores and homework."

"Okay," Danny replied, but made no move to comply.

Jarod glanced at the television, saw that a commercial was playing, then plucked the remote control off the coffee table and flipped the TV off.

"Hey!" Danny pivoted, glared over his shoulder. "I said okay. Don't rush me."

Susan's heart trembled at Jarod's thunderous expression. "Don't use that tone again, son." The words were issued quietly, which made them all the more intense. "Not with me, not with Susan, not with anyone. It's rude and disrespectful."

Danny's gaze darted from his father to Susan and back again, as if he was gauging his chances if he chose to push his father further. Opting for discretion, he stood without a word, scooped his textbooks from a nearby table and stomped into the kitchen.

As soon as Danny had left the room, Jarod's shoulders slumped slightly, and his eyes betrayed an exquisite sadness. "I apologize for my son's behavior lately. I don't know what has come over him."

It was the opening Susan had been waiting for. And fearing. "I think that I do." Every drop of moisture evaporated from her mouth. "We need to…talk."

Apprehension joined the sadness in Jarod's eyes. He glanced toward the kitchen, assuring himself that Danny was hunched over the table, engrossed in his schoolwork. "All right."

Inhaling deeply, Susan held the breath for courage, expelled it all at once. Claude yawned, gave her a reproachful stare as her awkward movements disturbed his slumber. The cat leaped down, and Susan grasped the stuffed arms of the lounge chair to push herself up.

In less than a heartbeat, Jarod crossed the room, gently took hold of her elbow to assist her. "It looks like the baby has dropped."

"Most definitely."

Jarod frowned. "Perhaps we should call the doctor. We don't have another appointment until the middle of next week."

The reminder that Jarod had attended every doctor appointment with her made Susan smile. "That shouldn't be necessary. During our last visit the doctor said the baby could turn into birthing position at any time during the final month."

Once she was standing, Susan cringed as a flurry of sharp pelvic pains competed with the throb of her abused feet.

Jarod slipped an arm around her, guided her toward his office. "Is there anything I can do to make you feel better?"

She shook her head, but managed a tenuous smile of thanks. Considering what she was about to tell him, a few physical discomforts were the least of her worries.

The expression on Susan's face was pained, pale. But not, Jarod realized, from the physical discomfort of advanced pregnancy. There was a wounding in her eyes. An emotional wounding. A pain too deep for tears.

It scared him half to death.

He guided her to the office sofa, steadied her as she lowered herself into the soft cushions. "You're doing too much," he said. "You should rest more."

She nodded, glanced away. "I'm fine."

Unconvinced, Jarod dragged a vinyl guest chair from beside the desk, and sat facing her. "I'll be going into Billings later this week. Is there anything I can bring you? Maybe you'd like to go along. There's a big mall, plenty of fancy shops for baby things, or—" he hesitated as a drop of moisture gathered on her lashes "—or something personal, maybe. You don't get out much since summer school ended. After the baby is born, it may be a while before you feel like going back to work. I don't want you to feel... isolated."

Like Gail did, he thought.

She shook her head. "I don't feel isolated, Jarod. I love the ranch. You know that."

Yes, he did know it. The stable hands had told him that she appeared every day to give treats to the horses and had even asked for lessons on how to curry and groom them. According to Elton, the senior hand, she'd been a bundle of excited questions, wanting to know everything about the ranch animals, everything about the ranch. She'd also peppered Jarod with questions over the past weeks, seeming exquisitely interested in every facet of the ranch itself and all related business interests from the feed-farming operation to equipment maintenance and the welding yard, which created the portable corrals and chutes required for herding cattle to market.

"Then maybe you'd just like to see a few city lights, have dinner in a nice restaurant? Lorraine Roundtree will watch Danny—"

"Jarod, we have to talk."

His heart sank. "All right."

She plucked a loose thread on the hem of her over-

size T-shirt. "I called Davis Grayson this morning."
She paused as if she actually heard the sudden thud
inside Jarod's chest, and was startled by it. After a
moment, she moistened her lips and continued. "I
asked him to proceed with alternative living arrangements for the baby and me."

Clamping his fingers over the chair's wooden arm-
rests, Jarod waited for the room to stop spinning. The
charade was over, he realized, the charade of a marriage that somewhere along the line had become real
to him. But clearly, it had not become real to Susan.

He leaned forward, pressing his hands against his
thighs to conceal the sudden tremor in his legs. "I
thought we...you decided that there was no rush in
finalizing those arrangements."

"I know." She spoke softly, avoided his gaze.
"Things have changed."

"What things?"

"My presence here," she whispered. "Things have
not gone the way I'd hoped." Her voice was so thin
that Jarod, positioned barely two feet away, had to lean
forward to hear her. "I've come between you and your
son, Jarod. I can't allow that to continue."

A dagger of truth twisted inside him, although he
refused to accept it. "That's as good an excuse as any,
I suppose."

Startled, she looked up. "It's not an excuse, Jarod.
I think you know that." Tears glistened in her eyes.
One slipped down her cheek, mute testimony to how
unhappy she was. How unhappy Jarod had made her.

"It doesn't matter." Standing quickly, Jarod
scraped the chair over the hardwood floor, nearly flung
it back into place beside the desk. "Now or two
months from now, that was always the plan, wasn't

it? Legalize the child, ensure her inheritance, then move on with your life.''

Her expression shattered him. "Yes, that was the plan.''

"Then you're simply adhering to the deal we made.'' He managed a bland shrug. "I won't go back on my word, if that's what concerns you. I'll expect the visitation we've agreed upon.''

"Yes, of course, but—''

"I want to play an important role in my child's life, a role beyond being a weekend dad whose only purpose is to supply a blank checkbook with which to purchase her affection.''

Susan actually flinched. It took all the self-discipline Jarod could muster not to gather her into his arms, and carry her with him for the rest of his life. Deep down he'd always known she would leave him. He wasn't an easy man to live with. He wasn't an easy man to love.

Love. That profound, enduring emotion that wraps itself around a lonely heart, and fills a cold void with warmth. Love existed without acknowledgment, without conscious recognition. Jarod understood that, even as he wondered exactly when it was that he'd fallen in love with this woman who was his wife, and why he hadn't recognized the depth of his feelings until it was too late.

He clasped his hands behind his back to keep from reaching for her. He could declare his love, plead with her to stay, but he had no right to do so. Even if she acquiesced to please him, she would be miserable, her spirit crushed, her independence destroyed. Jarod couldn't bear that, couldn't bear to hurt her.

He softened his tone. "I'll be a good father to our

daughter, Susan. I'll make certain you have everything you need to be safe and happy. Beyond that, I'll not interfere with your life. You have my word on that.''

She regarded him with exquisite sadness. Another tear slipped down her cheek, tore straight into his heart. He spun around, opened the office door.

''Wait.''

He hesitated without looking back.

''Please don't leave yet. We still have...issues.''

His fingers tightened around the door knob. ''Issues or not, I've got to set hay rolls on the grazing plains before first snow.''

Then Jarod strode out of the room, grabbed his jacket from the hook, and left the house before Susan had a chance to follow and glimpse the heartbreak in his eyes.

Susan emerged from the office feeling drained, empty. The roar of Jarod's truck became fainter, as distant as the expression in his eyes when she'd told him she'd be leaving.

He hadn't cared, had simply shrugged off her announcement as if it meant less than nothing to him. In fact, he'd probably been relieved by her decision. Jarod was too kind a man to have ever asked her to leave, even though it had been clear for weeks that her presence was destroying the fragile bond between him and his son.

Susan hadn't expected Jarod to experience the gut-wrenching grief that was ripping through her own soul. She had never fooled herself into believing that he returned the deep feelings she had for him. But she'd hoped he would at least express some hint of sadness, some small sense of loss.

She'd hoped that he would…care.

The slam of a door jarred her. She turned, realized the kitchen was empty at the same moment that Danny exploded from the hallway.

"I don't care if you go away," he cried. His eyes were red, his face flushed and wet with tears. "You never wanted to be my mom anyway. You were always gonna leave, just like she did."

"What?" Stunned, Susan glanced toward the office, and felt her heart thud inside her chest. "Good grief, sweetie, were you listening to your daddy and I talking? Were you listening several weeks ago, when Mr. Grayson was here?"

"You're gonna go away and take my baby sister, too, but I don't care. Sisters are stupid. Babies are lame." Sobbing, the child rushed past her and flung open the front door.

"Danny, wait! You're wrong, you don't understand—"

"I don't need you," he shouted. "I don't need anybody."

Before Susan could take two steps, the child had dashed out the door. The enormity of what she'd just learned crushed her. Everything made sense now. Danny's emotional withdrawal had begun the weekend that Davis Grayson had come to the ranch to discuss the terms of visitation and the eventual dissolution of a marriage that to Susan had become frighteningly real.

Clearly Danny had overhead the conversation and realized that Susan would soon abandon him, just as his real mother had. For a bewildered, heartsick little boy, the prospect of losing another mother had been too much to bear.

How could she have been so blind? Susan was intimately acquainted with the trauma of being repeatedly abandoned by a parent, the anger and emotional withdrawal coupled with fear of eventual loss. How could she have failed to recognize her own symptoms in the child she loved so deeply?

All she had ever wanted was to love and cherish this precious little boy, to make him feel safe and nurtured. Instead she had exacerbated his terror by contributing yet another parental abandonment to a fragile heart already wounded by loss.

Wind whipped through the open doorway, howling and frigid. Susan ducked into the gale, pushed her way onto the porch. "Danny? Danny, please come back!"

Squinting against the stinging wind, she surged forward, stumbled around the old barn to the place where Danny bounced his basketball and found solace when he was sad.

The crumpled form was hunched on the ground beneath the hoop that his father had finally erected for him. His sobs rose above the whistle of the wind. "Oh, Danny."

Bracing herself with one hand on the barn wall and the other cradling her belly, she painfully lowered herself beside the weeping child. "Sweetie, I know what you overheard. I understand how it must have sounded to you."

Danny sniffed, pulled away from the hand she laid on his small shoulder. "You're gonna leave."

She moistened her lips. "Eventually, yes. You're a big boy, Danny. You're old enough to understand the truth. I'm sorry we weren't honest with you." The words clogged in her throat, as painful to say as to hear aloud. "Your father and I got married because we wanted the very best for your baby sister. We agreed at the time it would be temporary, so you are right that I never planned on staying very long. But—'' she swallowed again, flinched against the deepening throb at the small of her back ''—but then something totally unexpected happened.''

Quaking with dry sobs, Danny glanced at her sideways. He wiped his nose with his shirt, squinted against the sting of the wind. ''What happened?''

''I fell in love with your father, Danny, and I fell in love with you. I didn't want to leave anymore. Not next month, not next year, not ever.''

A wary gladness lit his eyes, but only for a moment. ''But you're gonna leave. I heard you. You said you wanted to go away.''

''I don't want to, Danny, but I thought it would be best. I didn't know you had overheard our conversations. I thought your anger was caused by my presence, the fact that your dad didn't have as much time to spend with you. I was afraid the baby and I were destroying your relationship with your dad, and I just couldn't let that happen.''

''Uh-uh.'' Scrambling to his knees, he gazed up, seeming stunned by what she'd told him. ''I was only mad at Dad 'cause he was gonna let you go away. So now you can stay, right? Everything will be okay now?''

''I wish I could say yes, but it's not that simple.'' A sharp pain in her side made her gasp, shift positions. She caught her breath, bit her lip, and tried for a smile that didn't quite make it. ''Your father doesn't love me the way I love him, Danny. It's not fair for me to stay, and keep him from finding someone he could really love, someone who would be a real mom to you forever.''

A fresh spurt of tears splashed down the boy's cheeks, mingling with a few swirling snowflakes whipped by the howling storm. Susan flipped her head, tried to pushed the flyaway hair from her face. She blinked, tried to focus on Danny's face, and saw his lips moving but couldn't hear his voice. She felt odd, displaced, suddenly disoriented.

Then the pain struck, violent and crushing. She heard the gasp, the agonized scream rise above the raging storm. She felt the sting of pebbles against her face, and realized that she was lying on the cold earth. Wind-whipped snow pricked her face, numbed her hands. Pain tightened like a girdle of barbed wire, squeezing the breath out of her until she couldn't even scream any more. She knew Danny was shaking her arm, knew he was futilely attempting to drag her upright. She knew that her baby, her precious beloved child, was in desperate danger.

Then darkness slipped over her, and she knew nothing at all.

Chapter Thirteen

Red agony spiked through her belly, rousing her from frigid blackness. Completely disoriented, Susan reacted out of instinct, curling into a fetal position and cupping her hands beneath her stomach.

That's when she felt the icy wetness between her thighs, and knew that her water had broken. The cold seeped from her soaked maternity pants into her bones. Sharp stones from an earthen pillow pricked her cheek.

She didn't know where she was.

Beneath her face, the ground vibrated, a low rumble growing closer, closer, then becoming fainter, more distant, until it finally disappeared. Vague thoughts encircled her mind, hints of consciousness that desperately tried to breach the darkness. Her eyes opened, tiny slits stung by icy wind. She was outside, she realized. A dusting of snow coated the stark earth.

Something heavy covered her, something peculiar. She instinctively grasped it. A blanket.

She was outside, on the ground, in a snowstorm, covered with a blanket.

And the baby was coming.

Pressure built at the small of her back, encircled her like razor wire until her knees pulled up, and a cry of misery caught like a choked gurgle on the back of her tongue. Her breath came in sharp gasps. Fear bubbled as reality displayed itself to her awakening mind. She couldn't feel her feet. Her freezing, saturated pants numbed her thighs, and kept her body temperature dangerously low despite the blanket that mysteriously covered her.

She would lose consciousness soon. She would die soon.

And if she died, so would her child.

Desperate, Susan extended one arm, clawed at the cold ground, tried to propel forward with the feeble churning of numb legs and feet she could no longer feel. Her body heaved forward a few inches, then a few inches more.

She didn't know where she was going. She didn't know where she was. She knew only that staying was certain death. So she squirmed across the frigid ground like a stiff slug, inch by painful inch until the next pain hit and blackness claimed her once more.

Jarod pulled his glove off with his teeth, retrieved the wire cutters from his pocket and sliced the guide wires tying the huge rolls of cattle feed harvested only a few weeks ago.

Each roll was as tall as a man and would serve as a buffet for hungry cattle during the next few weeks.

If the snow piled deep enough to cover the hay rolls, smaller bales would be dropped from the air to tide the herd through spring. Most of the cattle had been trucked to market a few weeks earlier. Only the breeding females and their half-grown offspring would weather the cruelest season. Winter was the toughest part of ranching. Weather was an unpredictable—and harsh—enemy.

Samuel rumbled up in his old pickup, exited and strode toward Jarod in the banty-legged style that was so uniquely his own. The old foreman puckered a frown at the hundreds of hay rolls set up across the first segment of the ten thousand acres used as winter grazing for the remaining herd.

"The boys are moving the first batch of heifers and yearlings down from the mesa." Samuel spat on the ground, then regarded the activity of several ranch hands cutting wire and splitting bales. "Got a good crop of winter feed this year."

"We'll need it." Tugging his hat down against the wind, Jarod squinted toward the northwest. "Got a howler coming. There will probably be six inches of snow on the ground by morning, a foot by tomorrow night."

"We got the ranch snowplows pulled from the maintenance yard, ready to clear the roads soon as the storm passes." Shrugging his shoulders, Samuel pulled up the fleece-lined collar of his ranch coat. "How's your missus doing?"

Although the polite query twisted inside his chest, Jarod kept his expression absolutely even. There was no way he would share his private pain, not even with a friend. "Doing fine, Samuel."

Samuel studied him with wise, rheumy eyes. "Last

few weeks are tough on a momma. Sometimes hard to cope.''

Jarod felt a muscle in his jaw betray him with a twitch. ''Heard from Martha lately?''

It was a deliberate change of topic that Samuel thankfully respected. ''She called last night. Said she'll be home in a day or two.''

A nuance in the old man's voice jarred Jarod out of his private misery. ''Is her sister feeling better?''

Samuel chewed, spat, wiped his mouth with his jacket sleeve. ''Ethel done passed on yesterday.''

''I'm sorry.''

''She was a good woman. Martha's taking it poorly.''

''Is there anything I can do? Does the family need help with...expenses?''

''Doubt it. Services are set for tomorrow.''

''You should go, Samuel. I'll call our travel agent, and have you booked on the next flight.''

''Ain't nothing moving 'til this here storm passes. By then Martha will be on her way.'' Samuel shrugged. ''She's a strong woman, don't need the likes of me propping her up—'' The old man stopped mid-sentence, squinted toward a faraway ridge line. ''Who in tarnation is that fool? He's gonna kill that poor horse.''

Jarod followed Samuel's gaze, saw the frosted breath of an animal being pushed to the edge of endurance by a rider who was clearly no expert. Jarod swore, took two steps forward, then froze in his tracks, recognizing the golden mare a moment before Samuel spoke.

''Holy hell,'' Samuel muttered. ''Ain't that Buttermilk? What the devil is Elton thinking, riding that poor animal into the ground like that? Ain't even got her saddled, by God. I'll have his bloody hide, I will—''

''That's not Elton.'' Terror gripped Jarod's spine, crushed the breath from his lungs. The small rider hunched forward until his face brushed Buttermilk's ivory mane, bouncing with every precarious stride until it seemed only sheer force of will kept him from being thrown to the snowy ground.

By the time Jarod's mind acknowledged what his eyes had confirmed, he'd bolted forward and was sprinting across the barren plain to meet the exhausted animal and its terrified rider.

Jarod took the bridle. Buttermilk whinnied, pranced sideways, breathing hard. ''Calm down, girl, shh, okay now, you're fine.'' The mare was sweating profusely. Steam puffed from her flaring nostrils, foam dripped from her mouth. Her eyes were wide, rolling with fear and confusion, her chest heaved with every tortured breath.

Samuel loped up, muttering, and took the reins, freeing Jarod to grasp the terrified child still clinging to the mare's back.

Danny opened his eyes the moment his father took hold of him. ''D-dad!'' He flung his arms around Jarod's neck, shivered violently. ''I was so scared we wouldn't find you.''

Jarod hugged him fiercely. ''You could have killed yourself. You're not strong enough to ride. Your leg—''

''It's Mom,'' the boy blurted. ''The baby is coming.''

Every drop of blood seemed to drain from Jarod's body. He swayed, clinging even more tightly to his freezing, terrified child.

"She hurts real bad," Danny said between gulps of air. "She fell down outside and couldn't get up and the phone doesn't work and I didn't know what to do so I c-came to find you and—" he sucked more air, tears spurted from his eyes "—and I'm scared she's gonna die, Dad, I'm so scared she's gonna die."

Samuel swore, balled the reins in his fist. "Take the young'un and go," he said. "The boys and me will finish up here."

But Jarod was already running toward the truck with his son in his arms. It was the culmination of his worst nightmare. Another woman he loved was in desperate trouble, medical help was hours away and Jarod wasn't there. Again.

Fear clawed like a demonic beast, gashing through his heart and his soul. Jarod drove like a madman. The pickup sped and slid over snow-covered roads, bounced across rutted paths, fishtailed around dangerous hairpin curves while the weather deteriorated. The storm increased in intensity with snow piling on the windshield faster than the wipers could push it aside.

Danny, clad only in a thin jacket and blue jeans, hunched on the bench seat, whimpering. His eyes were huge, dark, filled with anguish. Jarod could have wept, wept with gratitude at the bravery of a youngster who'd overcome his own terror to seek help for the stepmother he loved; wept with bitter remorse that his own failures as a father, as a husband, had once again brought grief and despair to everyone he cared about.

Teeth chattering, Danny hugged himself, stared out at the storm. "I put a blanket on her," he mumbled. "Do you think that will keep her warm enough so she won't freeze and stuff?"

"Of course it will." Jarod swallowed panic at the image of his beloved Susan lying unconscious on the ground in a raging snowstorm, covered only by a thin blanket. "You did everything right, son, everything exactly right."

Danny chewed his lower lip. "I tried to call the emergency number, like you told me. The phone wouldn't work."

"I know." Phone lines usually went down during storms. Too many miles of wire stretched over too much wilderness. Just another inconvenience of ranch life, he thought bitterly. Isolation, loneliness, the destruction of everyone he loved…all inconveniences of a lifestyle that was as much a part of Jarod as his blood and his bones.

"How come you're gonna make Mom go away?"

"What?" Jarod jerked the wheel to avoid a rut, then swung the truck back onto the road. "I'm not going to make her go away."

"I heard you," Danny insisted. "That Mr. Grayson fellow was talking about Mom moving after the baby comes, and this morning you acted like you didn't care if she went away."

A cold chill slipped down his spine. "You heard that?"

"Yeah." His voice was thin, dull. "I got real mad. I yelled at her and stuff. I said bad things." Sniffing, he turned his face away, dabbed his eyes. "She told me not to go outside, but I did anyway. So she came out, too, and explained all about how you guys got married on account of the baby, and how she had to leave because you don't love her the way she loves you."

Danny continued to mumble, but Jarod was no

longer listening. The shock of what he'd just learned still reverberated through every fiber of his body.

...you don't love her the way she loves you.

He loved her more than his next breath, more than life itself. He loved her more than the ranch, which was more a part of him than the blood in his veins. How could Susan not know that? How could she not understand the depth of surging emotion flooding his heart every time she smiled, every time she gazed in his direction, every time she giggled at a silly joke or tousled his son's hair? How could she not feel the heat of desire coursing through his veins at her slightest touch, how could she not recognize the love in his words, his eyes, his touch?

Epiphany struck with a voice from his past, the voice of a wise father counseling his receptive son. "Women judge a man by his deeds, not his words. A real man don't go around sniveling about how much he loves his woman. Hell, she already knows that. A real man takes care of business. Women appreciate that, Jarod, they surely do." The vision of his father's weathered face appeared like a specter in Jarod's mind. "Just take care of business, son. Everything else takes care of itself."

That was exactly how Vernon Bodine had led his life, Jarod realized. Never once had he said the words *I love you,* not to Jarod's mother, not to Jarod.

And Jarod was his father's son.

Simple words, the most powerful on earth. Jarod had never uttered them in his life.

"Dad, watch out!"

Instinctively Jarod twisted the wheel, hit the brake. The pickup truck skidded and spun. Metal crunched, steel shattered. Then the storm embraced them.

* * *

A keening cry broke the howl of the wind, an anguished scream of a wounded beast. Susan listened from a place outside herself, oddly displaced from the pitiful creature writhing on the snow-covered ground. The pathetic thrashing she witnessed seemed to serve no purpose beyond the most basic primal instinct.

Vaguely aware that a birthing was in progress, Susan was mildly intrigued, but felt no immediacy, no sense of crisis. Instead she hovered at a place beyond her mind, a calm vantage point from which she observed a body she knew to be her own with peculiar apathy.

Clearly the physical vessel was experiencing extreme trauma. The legs flopped almost comically each time the enormous belly knotted with spasms. The contorted face was white as death except for one cheek that was abraded raw, beaded with drops of frozen blood. The lips were an unflattering shade of blue.

Not her finest moment, she decided, and wondered why she felt no sense of urgency, no gut-wrenching fear. There was no pain where she was now. Viewing the scene with complacent objectivity, she knew what the woman on the ground could not know her journey was futile. The useless blanket lay discarded where it was fallen, some twenty feet away. Death was inevitable now, for the woman. For the child.

The child.

A strange stirring swirled through the odd specter that was herself, a troubling surge of emotion that was out of place in the contented plane on which she hovered. The baby, her baby, had no choice. Giving in to the comfort of death meant depriving a helpless infant of a chance to live, to grow, to learn and love and give birth to her own children some day.

Images circled Susan's mind, visions of a dancing girl with her daddy's gray eyes, a daughter that would never exist unless her mother fought to survive.

The images blurred into a vortex of darkness. And she willingly returned to the pain.

"She was here, Dad!" Ducking into the wind, Danny limped to the abandoned blanket, his small face a mask of confusion, and fear. "Maybe she woke up and went into the house?"

"Maybe," Jarod mumbled, although he didn't believe it. The storm was nearing blizzard strength. Visibility vacillated from a few inches to a few feet. "Hold on to my belt, son. Don't let go, no matter what."

When Jarod felt the boy's small, shivering fingers press against the small of his back, he squinted at the ground, following drag marks in the snow. Somehow she had managed to crawl to the edge of the barn, and around the corner. Something inside Jarod cracked, shattered.

Deep down, he knew it was too late. No one could survive in this, not even a woman as strong and determined as his beloved Susan. He wanted to fall to his knees screaming, to hurl epithets at a world cruel enough to crush all that was innocent and precious.

Bracing himself on the side of the barn, he struggled forward, step after painful step until the faint outline of a form appeared in the distance. Ignoring the terror of what he would find, he slogged onward, knelt beside her and nearly wept.

She was alive. Barely.

Jarod lifted her gently, shifted to accommodate her weight. "Hold on," he murmured, to both the moaning woman in his arms and the struggling child clinging to his belt. "We're almost there. Just hold on."

Her eyes fluttered open. "Our b-baby." The hoarse whisper broke between chattering teeth. "H-help her."

"I will," he vowed.

A sigh slipped out on a breath, and she was silent.

Ducking into the brutal wind, Jarod struggled forward carrying his wife and unborn child while his son hobbled behind him, clinging desperately to his belt.

When they finally reached the safety of the house, he rushed Susan to the nearest bed, which was in the guest room. Behind him, Danny hovered with worried eyes. "Turn up the heat, son. If the electricity is out, hit the generator switch. You know how."

The boy nodded, disappeared from the doorway while Jarod frantically stripped off Susan's wet clothing, and covered her with warm blankets. As he massaged her icy feet and legs, he heard his son's limping footsteps on the hardwood floors.

"Should I, like, boil water or something?"

Jarod glanced over his shoulder, swallowed a lump of emotion at the brave young man who was his son. "That's a good idea. She might be able to sip some warm tea."

"Tea?" Danny looked at the moaning woman, frowned. "Is that what they do with the boiled water?"

"Is that what who does with it?"

He shrugged. "I dunno, but whenever ladies get ready to have babies in movies and stuff, someone always runs to boil water. I never figured it was to drink.''

"Ah.'' Pleased by the pink color returning to Susan's feet, Jarod covered them with a blanket and moved up to massage each of her arms. ''I've always thought that boiling water was just a way to keep men busy so they didn't get in the way of the real work.''

"Oh.'' The boy shifted his stance, flinched slightly.

It was a subtle expression, but Jarod noticed. ''Your leg is hurting again, isn't it?''

"It's okay.''

They both knew that although the injury had been healing well, the bones still weren't strong enough for the grueling ordeal of a frantic horseback ride, and a quarter-mile hike from the gully where the disabled pickup was stuck. ''Change your wet clothes, son, then use your cane to keep some of the weight off your leg.''

Danny's gaze was riveted on Susan. ''Is she gonna be okay, Dad?''

"She's going to be fine.'' Jarod prayed that was true.

A low moan filtered from somewhere deep inside her. She curled forward, gasping.

Jarod slipped an arm under her shoulders, held her tight. ''That's good, honey, you're doing good.'' The words rang hollow in his own ears, but instinct told him that she needed to hear them. ''That's right, hold on, the pain will ease in a few minutes.''

Her face went from white to pink to crimson. Her mouth opened, but no sound came out.

A memory from Danny's birth flashed into his mind, instructions a nurse had whispered while he'd held Gail's hand in the delivery room. ''Breathe, Su-

san...short breaths, like a panting dog...like this.''
Jarod demonstrated until he felt light-headed. Susan
seemed not to notice, but after a moment she fell back
against the pillow, sucked a wheezing breath, then began to pant obediently.

He smiled, brushed the hair from her face.

She managed to smile back. Her teeth weren't chattering any more, and the sickly blue tint had faded
from her lips. ''You're not a dream this time, are you?
You're really here.''

''I'm here, honey. I'm here.''

Her smile faded. ''Danny. Dear God, Danny—''
She pressed her elbows into the mattress, tried to push
upright.

''Danny's fine, he's just fine.'' Jarod nodded at the
boy, who stumbled forward, looking terrified. ''He's
right here.''

''Oh-h-h.'' Tears moistened her eyes. She reached
weakly out to touch the boy's face. ''I've been so
worried.''

Danny blinked in surprise. ''About me?''

Her hand dropped to the mattress as if it weighed a
million pounds. ''I couldn't...find you.''

Jarod continued to caress her forehead. Her skin was
still cool and moist, but no longer felt icy. ''That's
because he was riding Buttermilk up to the north mesa
to get help.''

Comprehension dawned slowly, and she widened
her eyes. ''You...rode? For me?'' The tears gathered
in her eyes, slipped down her cheeks and soaked into
the pillow. ''That was so brave,'' she whispered.
''You are my hero.''

Danny actually blushed.

Susan cried out, grabbed Jarod's hand. The pain enveloped her, seeming even stronger than the last. He comforted her as best he could until she fell back, gasping, sobbing, terrified.

He read the question in her eyes. "We can't make it to the hospital in time. The truck is ditched at the edge of the driveway, and the storm is too fierce for an ambulance to get to us." A glaze of despair veiled her gaze. Jarod touched her cheek, urging her to look at him. "Samuel knows what's happening, honey. He'll bring help as soon as he can."

"Our baby…is coming."

"Yes, our baby is coming." Saying the words aloud gave Jarod palpitations. "And I'm going to be blessed with the privilege of delivering our daughter."

Her eyes widened, then narrowed. "Have you done this before?"

"Sure," he lied.

"How many times where the patient didn't have hooves?"

He shrugged. "Well, if you're going to get picky—"

She lurched upright, screaming. Jarod held her shoulders, massaged the small of her back, and prayed.

"Should I go get the come-along?" Danny asked helpfully.

"No, son." Jarod lowered Susan back onto the pillows. "Babies aren't pulled out with winches the way some calves are." With unexpected expertise Jarod arranged the covers to make a tent over her knees, braced her feet against the footboard, and tried to send Danny out of the room. "Go see to that hot water, will you please? I'll come get you if we need anything."

"Is the baby coming?"

"Yes, son."

"But I should stay. You might need help, you know, like you did when Buttermilk had her foal. I brought you stuff you needed." The boy sounded desperate, as if he might cry. "I can get you towels. Do you need towels? And Mom needs me, she needs to hold on to me when it hurts too bad."

To reinforce that, Danny dashed to the head of the bed and grasped Susan's hand. Panting, obviously weak, she still managed a smile for him. "I'm afraid I'll squeeze you too hard."

"I'm tough," the boy informed her. "Bodines are always tough."

Jarod was so proud he could have exploded. Proud of the son who had overcome his own fear to save a woman he loved; proud of his beloved wife, who displayed a courage that humbled him.

Surrounded by bravery, Jarod had no choice but to deal with the terror gnawing deep in his own gut. He sucked a breath, felt an icy calm slip over him like a shroud. He could do this. He *would* do this.

A thin cry captured his attention. Susan grasped Danny's hand, curled forward like a shrimp. She panted through clenched teeth, her face contorted.

Suppressing an urge to leap to her side, Jarod steadied her quivering thighs and saw the bulge of a small head appear a moment before she fell back, gasping and exhausted. Another contraction hit within seconds. "Push," Jarod said. "Push as hard as you can."

He cupped his hands around the infant's head as it emerged, and realized in horror that the umbilical cord was wrapped around the baby's neck.

A bad situation had just become immeasurably worse.

Chapter Fourteen

Susan was cold again. The blessed warmth that had silenced her chattering teeth now dissipated with every agonizing contraction until the bone-chilling cold enveloped her from the inside out.

The pressure was enormous, as if her entire body was crushed by an ever-tightening vise. She'd lost all control of her muscles, was alternately curled forward by rock-hard spasms then flung backward, gasping and limp, as if she were a rag doll. Lights flashed inside her skull. The room spun wildly. Voices echoed from the paradox of near distance.

Tense voices, troubled voices. Frightened voices.

"Get those towels for me, as many as you can carry."

"What's happening, Dad? Why is Mom so white? Why isn't the baby coming out?"

"Bring the sewing kit, too."

A choked scream flung Susan forward. Shades of crimson flashed behind her tightly closed lids.

"Push!"

The command was urgent, hoarse.

"Push, Susan, push as hard as you can."

Her body was already pushing, the invisible vise ratcheting pressure until she feared she would burst.

"I know it's hard, honey, but you have to try."

The pain would have been unbearable if she'd allowed herself to endure it. Pain was overwhelmed by the pressure, the exquisite sensation of being forcefully folded inside out.

"A little more...that's it...you're doing good, so good." His voice thinned to a hoarse murmur. "Oh, God."

The horror expressed in those two words sliced her like a blade. Something was wrong, dreadfully wrong. The baby.

The baby.

A surge of strength pulsed from somewhere outside herself, a sudden burst of determined effort exploded from force of sheer will. She gritted her teeth, concentrated every ounce of strength on the task of bringing her precious child into the world.

"That's it! She's coming, honey...she's coming. *Push!*"

Susan's body seemed to explode, then suddenly unwound like a loosed spring. She collapsed with a wheezing gasp. Odd little hee-hee sounds whistled from between her teeth. The room kept spinning. She was nauseous.

And she was so very, very cold.

"Put the towels down there." Tension edged

Jarod's voice, a preoccupied tautness that circled her fuzzy mind.

A fragile, trembling answer pulled Susan from the brink of unconsciousness. "I can't find the sewing kit, Dad, I can't find it! How come the baby's head is that funny color? Is the baby gonna die?"

"No." The response was terse, firm. Unconvincing.

"But Mom looks all sick and stuff...please, Daddy, don't let Mom die. Don't let my baby sister die."

"Nobody is going to die, son. Nobody." The determination in his voice soothed Susan, gave her another surge of strength. "The sewing kit is in the hall closet. Get it quickly."

Susan heard the echo of fast footsteps on hardwood, then was yanked forward with the next contraction.

"Push, Susan, push as hard as you can!"

Susan concentrated on that voice, coiled forward until her chin touched her chest and pushed until the splashes of light behind her squinched lids darkened to crimson, then scarlet, and finally faded to black.

Awareness dawned slowly, with vague sounds filtering into the soft fabric of an awakening mind.

The muted howl of the wind outside. The distant thump of a loose shutter. The echo of footsteps, small and quick.

"This one's all hot, Dad."

A shuffle, a light swish of air, as if someone had moved close. She was suddenly enveloped by delicious warmth. A sigh of pure ecstasy slipped from her parched lips.

"Put another blanket in the dryer, son, so it will be ready when this one cools."

"I already did." The sweet, familiar young voice

was closer now. A small, warm hand touched her forehead. "She's whiter than that old tomcat that used to sneak around bugging Claude. How come she won't wake up?"

"Having a baby is hard work, Danny, the hardest work in the world. She needs to rest."

Having a baby.

Baby.

The thought of her child roused a mind perched on the precipice of consciousness. She moaned, struggled to lift eyelids that seemed to weigh a thousand pounds each.

Baby. Her baby. Their baby.

She heard it then, a faint snuffle barely discernible between the howl of the wind and the rhythmic thud of the shutter. A tiny fuss, a squeaky squall, a cranky mew, not unlike that of a hungry kitten.

A baby. Her baby. Their baby.

With a surge of strength that stunned her, Susan opened her eyes. Two blurred figures hovered over her, one large, one small. A whisper emerged, a voice she barely recognized as her own. "Our...baby?"

The larger figure bent closer, pressed a kiss on her forehead, then straightened and moved away from the bed. A prickle of panic skittered across her nape. She blinked to clear her vision, instinctively tried to sit up, fighting the heated blanket tucked tightly around her.

Within the space of a heartbeat, Jarod returned and laid a wrapped bundle on her tummy. Susan gasped in awe and in joy. A tiny pink face framed by feathers of dark hair peered from the blanket cocoon, curious eyes blinking open, then squinching shut as the perfect rosebud mouth stretched into a yawn.

Jarod bent to kiss the infant's scalp. "Meet your

mommy, sweetheart,'' he whispered. ''Your wonderful, wonderful mommy.''

''Oh.'' Tears sprang to Susan's eyes. She struggled to extract her arms from beneath the blanket, reached out to caress the exquisitely soft little cheek with her fingertip. The infant immediately turned toward the touch with her tiny, grasping mouth. ''Oh, she is so precious.''

Danny shifted. ''Yeah, well she looks okay now. Dad cleaned her up and stuff. She was gross when she first came out, all wrinkled and gooey.'' He shuddered adorably.

Susan could have kissed him until he sputtered. ''You saved your sister's life.''

Danny blushed. ''I didn't do nothing.''

''You did everything.'' Susan remembered the vibration of earth beneath her cheek, the rumble that had grown closer, then more distant. Hoofbeats, she now realized. ''You were so brave, Danny, so very courageous. I don't know of anyone on earth who could have overcome his own fear with such selfless determination.''

Clearly uncomfortable, yet pleased by the praise, Danny fidgeted with the silken hem of the warm blanket. ''Buttermilk did all the hard work.'' The boy's gaze slipped to the infant. He smiled. ''Dad says she's got your funny pout-dimple and my chin.''

''Pout-dimple?''

''Yeah, you know, that dent in the corner of your mouth when you get upset about stuff.''

Susan was unaware of the dimple in question but found the information to be enormously amusing. She giggled giddily, overwhelmed by sheer joy.

''The pout-dimple is an attractive plus,'' Jarod said.

"Unfortunately, she also has my eyebrows. Not so attractive, and not much of a plus."

"I adore your eyebrows," Susan whispered.

"Much as I appreciate the support, I doubt our daughter will be thrilled to look like she has a pair of hairy caterpillars crawling across her forehead."

Jarod moved the infant to the crook of Susan's arm, whereupon Susan greedily unwrapped the precious package and began a meticulous inspection of each tiny finger and toe. The infant was perfectly formed with a round tummy and fleshy little legs, weighing about seven and a half to eight pounds, considerably more than Susan would have expected of a baby born two weeks early. Her skin was a healthy shade of pink tinged with the dusky violet of a newborn. She was alert, clearly curious, and gazed up with eyes that seemed utterly focused, although Susan was well aware that her optical awareness was limited to movement and light.

Jarod watched with a proud smile. "Elisa Jane is a pretty little thing, isn't she? I mean, considering the fact that she will probably demand eyebrow tweezers by her second birthday."

Susan laughed. "Tiffany Dior will not be tweezing anything until she is at least sixteen. Until then she will have to be content with a handsome, if somewhat bushy frame for those cute little peepers."

Danny's perplexed gaze moved from Jarod to Susan. "How come you have so many names for her?"

"Her name is Tiffany Dior," Susan insisted.

Jarod offered an exaggerated sigh. "I don't care if she inherited your pout-dimple or the shape of your eyes, but I sure hope she didn't inherit your stubbornness."

"Tiffany Dior is a perfectly fine name."

"For a jewelry store."

Danny reached out, tickled the palm of the baby's hand and giggled when the infant promptly clamped hold of his finger. "I think we should call her Samantha."

"Why Samantha?" Susan asked.

Jarod's eyes took on a soft glow. "Samantha was my mother's name."

Smiling, Susan cupped her palm around the baby's softly furred little head. "My mother's name was Jean."

Jarod sat on the edge of the mattress, gently so as not to jostle mother and child. He gazed lovingly upon his daughter's face. "Samantha Jean Bodine. I like it."

"So do I," Susan murmured. On cue the infant kicked her feet, flailed an arm and emitted a baby gurgle. "I guess it's unanimous."

Susan's heart swelled until she feared it might burst. Flashes from the birthing process strobed through her mind, along with twinges of the fear she'd felt. She hugged the infant close, blinked back another surge of moisture.

She grasped Jarod's hand. "Thank you," she whispered. "If not for you, I don't know what I would have done."

A peculiar glaze veiled his eyes. "If not for me, you would have given birth in a safe, warm hospital, and our baby wouldn't have been subjected to inept fumbling more likely to cause harm than prevent it."

The leashed anger in his voice gave her pause. "You saved us both." He shook his head. She continued as if she hadn't noticed. "I don't know exactly what happened, but I do know that the baby was in trouble and you saved her.''

''You were the one who saved her, Susan. You were at death's door, going into shock, and you still managed to summon the strength to deliver in time for the umbilical cord to be untangled before it cut off blood supply to her brain.''

The horrific image made Susan catch her breath. A tremor slipped down her spine, through her limbs.

''You're cold again,'' Danny announced, clearly distressed. ''Maybe the other blanket is all warm now.'' He spun on his sneakers and dashed out of the room.

Shifting position, Jarod caressed the infant's head, then cupped Susan's hand between his strong, calloused palms. ''I thought I was going to lose you both.'' A weary shudder thinned his voice, stark contrast to the confident strength usually exuded when he spoke. ''I'm going to sell the ranch.''

The statement was so utterly unexpected that it took a moment for its impact to affect Susan. Slowly, cautiously she raised her gaze from the baby and looked at Jarod's tormented face. ''You can't do that. This ranch means everything to you.''

''No, it doesn't. It doesn't mean as much to me as my son, who despises living here with every fiber of his body. It doesn't mean as much to me as my daughter, who could have been damaged for life because I couldn't provide the medical care she needed. It doesn't mean as much to me as you do, Susan, you who have become center of my entire world.'' He paused, raised her hand to his lips and kissed her fingertips. ''The ranch has always come first with me. I never admitted that, couldn't even really see it. But today, when you nearly died because I hadn't been there when you needed me, something just cracked inside. I realized that if I never set foot on Sky View soil again, I'd survive. But if I ever lost you or Danny or—'' his tormented gaze dropped to the bright-eyed infant ''—or Samantha...well, I couldn't survive. And I wouldn't want to.''

A lump wedged in Susan's throat, cutting off the spill of words clogging behind it. She tried to speak, but couldn't. Instead, a fresh slip of tears welled in her eyes.

Jarod took a breath, clutched her hand. ''I'm not good at this, honey, so be patient with me. Bodines have always been a tight-lipped bunch, arrogant enough to presume that everyone knew what we were thinking so there was never any reason to duplicate the effort with real words. I figured you understood...that you realized how much you meant to me. I figured you knew how much I loved you.''

A thin sheen of perspiration glowed on his forehead.

''You...love me?''

''I do.'' He coughed, took a deep breath. ''I love you with all my heart, with all my soul. I know I've been a failure as a husband, but if you'll give me another chance I promise to do whatever it takes to make you happy.''

It was too much to comprehend. He loved her, he actually loved her enough to sacrifice everything dear to him for her sake, and the sake of his children. ''Ranching is in your blood. Your father was born here. You were born here. Your children were born here. It's your home.''

''Home is anywhere my family can be safe and happy.''

"You can't sell the ranch!" Danny blurted from the doorway. The child rushed into the room with a wadded, fresh-from-the-dryer blanket in his arms. He looked frightened, almost panicked. "Where would we go, how would we live?"

Jarod pivoted on the edge of the mattress, faced his wide-eyed son. "We can move into town, be closer to your school, your friends. That would make you happy, wouldn't it?"

The boy's lips quivered. "Where would Buttermilk live? How would Thunder know where to find us when he finally comes home?"

A befuddled expression creased Jarod's brow, followed by a poignant smile that touched Susan's heart. "Do you want Thunder to come home, Danny?"

The child sniffed, shrugged, muttered. "If he wants to, it's okay. Like, he didn't really mean to be bad."

Jarod's eyes reddened. He blinked, turned away. The significance of what had just occurred was not lost on Susan. By offering forgiveness to the half-wild mustang that had nearly taken his young life, Danny was also absolving his father of the blame and anger that had seethed inside since the accident. And the forgiveness went even further, she realized. Danny no longer blamed his father for the death of his mother.

With his son's forgiveness, perhaps now Jarod could finally forgive himself.

It took a moment for Jarod to speak. When he did, his voice was tender, raw with emotion. "We'll find a good home for Buttermilk, son, and Thunder too."

Not totally mollified, Danny continued to chew his lower lip. His gaze darted from his father to Susan and the baby. "Do we have to go away?"

"I thought you wanted to."

"I did. I mean, I do, I guess." Frowning, he crossed the room, piled the warm blanket on the foot of the bed. He fingered the warm fleece, spoke to Susan without looking at her. "Are you and Samantha gonna come, too?"

Susan moistened her dry lips, shook her head slowly. "No."

Beside her, the mattress dipped as Jarod shifted around. His crestfallen expression was quickly concealed, but not quickly enough. "I understand," he said quietly.

"Actually, I don't think you do understand." Susan scooped Samantha into her arms. The infant was startled by the movement, shifted her bright gaze to absorb this new perspective. "As long as we are married, half of this ranch is legally mine, true?"

Jarod offered a somber nod.

"Well, I don't intend to sell my half, nor do I intend to leave it. Samantha and I will be right here." She glanced at two stunned male faces, one large, one small. "You are both welcome to visit us any time, of course. Or..." she paused for effect "...or you could stay here and continue to run the Sky View Ranch like proper Bodines."

While comprehension dawned slowly in Jarod's eyes, Susan held out her hand to Danny, who immediately scrambled onto the opposite side of the bed and threw his arms around her neck.

"I love you both so much," Susan whispered, hugging Danny with her right arm, while the curious infant gazed up from the crook of her left elbow. "I never believed that I'd ever find a prince of my own. Instead I found two of them, galloping into my life not on a white stallion, but on a golden mare. I am the luckiest woman on earth.''

Danny loosened his grip, scooted onto his knees beside her. ''So you're gonna stay forever and ever and ever?''

''You couldn't drive me away with a stick.'' Smiling, Susan dabbed her moist eyes, surprised by the sudden laughter burbling from her throat. ''We are a family. Families stay together no matter what.'' She turned toward Jarod, her voice softening with love and an emotion so deep it frightened her. ''We are also Bodines. This ranch is our history, and the legacy we leave to our children and our children's children.''

Reaching out, Jarod traced the contours of Susan's face with his thumb, a touch so sweet, so enduring, that she nearly wept with sheer joy. ''I love you, Mrs. Bodine.''

''And I love you, Mr. Bodine, more than you will ever know.''

From his vantage point on the windowsill, Claude observed the peculiar scene with curious cat eyes, then returned his attention to the view beyond the frosty glass.

Outside, the howl of the wind softened into a sigh. Silent snow blanketed Bodine land. Seasons were changing. Mice would be scarce until spring. Still, the house was warm, the humans were happy. Claude settled his chin on his paws, and purred.

Epilogue

The warm summer day pulsed with activity, vibrated with a cacophony of happy sounds. Squealing children dashed between the clusters of chatting adults and the vibrant colors of Gail's garden blossoming beside the old barn. Beyond the house, horses snorted and whinnied, raising dust as the Roundtree teens raced their mounts from the stables to the edge of the mesa and back again.

Danny wasn't riding today, although he had slowly resumed his lessons on Buttermilk. He and Jarod often rode to the catfish pond beside the feed fields, but today the youngster simply cheered the racers on, pausing to provide occasional commentary to the bright-eyed infant seated in a nearby stroller.

Susan presumed Danny was offering big-brother explanations of the equine activity, since eight-month-old Samantha had never witnessed a horse race.

As Susan paused on the porch to admire the gathering of friends and family, her eldest sister emerged from a group of laughing women that included Martha West and Lorraine Roundtree.

"Another platter of sandwiches?" Laura said as Susan descended the porch steps. "Wow, you Montanans sure know how to party."

Stepping around Claude, who was stretched in a patch of sunshine on the first porch step, Susan set the plate of food on a picnic table already laden with delectable goodies. "We hay-sucking yahoos with dung on our boots just love a celebration. Right, Lorraine?"

Lorraine emitted an ear-shattering cross between a cackle and a guffaw. "Taught her well, Marty! Danged if she ain't one of us for sure."

Martha smiled, rolled her eyes. "Aye, roughened those citified edges, we have."

"Whatever you've done to my sister, it agrees with her," Laura said. "I've never seen her so radiant."

"Hey now, we ain't taking credit for that. Talk to old Jarod about that cat-with-cream-on-its-whiskers grin." Lorraine jerked a thumb backwards toward the broad-shouldered rancher walking his two brothers-in-law up toward the stables. "Jarod's the one who took teacher back to school for some private lessons. Right, hon?"

Lorraine playfully elbowed Susan's ribs, then emitted a guttural whoop that made Susan smile and Laura wince.

The slam of the screen door caught Susan's attention. Catrina waddled onto the porch, shading her eyes and cupping her swollen tummy with her free hand. "What was that god-awful noise? Did someone just butcher a pig?"

Martha snorted. "The song of a slaughtered hog is but a soft croon compared to the screech of a big-mouthed Roundtree."

Lorraine feigned umbrage, although her dark eyes glittered with humor. "Ain't nothing wrong with a hearty Montana giggle."

"Giggle?" Catrina wiped the sleep from her eyes, anxiously studied the scampering group of youngsters dashing around the yard. Only when she'd spotted her four-year-old daughter Heather did the apprehension seep from her eyes. "More like a bestial death scream."

"You city folks just don't appreciate a good belly laugh." Issuing a good-natured harrumph, Lorraine snagged Martha's elbow. "Let's go harass the men-folk for a while, and let these gals catch up on family matters."

Smiling, Susan returned to the porch, slipped an affectionate arm around her youngest sister's shoulders. "How was your nap?"

Catrina flushed. "I just meant to close my eyes for a moment."

"Pregnant folks need rest," Laura said, joining her siblings on the porch. "Rick, the ever-doting love of your life, gave specific instructions that you were not to be disturbed."

"He didn't!"

"Oh, but he did." Susan glanced toward the three men still sauntering up the stable road. "I like your husband, Cat. It's clear he adores you and Heather. Rick is a fine man."

A fluid warmth darkened Catrina's eyes. "He's my prince," she whispered. "My very own prince."

Laura was also gazing toward the group of men with

reverence. "Rick is terrific," she agreed. "Almost as wonderful as my Royce. Now when comparing princes—"

Susan interrupted. "When comparing princes, Jarod wins, hands-down."

"Does not," Laura insisted.

Grinning, Susan lightly shouldered her sister, a nostalgic replay of the gleeful manner in which the siblings aggravated each other as children. "Does too."

Mischief illuminated Laura's bright eyes. "Does—" she gently pinched her sister's arm "—not!"

"Ouch! Oh, you've asked for it now—"

Catrina sighed, perfectly mimicking their mother's exasperated tone. "Girls, girls, girls."

Susan and Laura replied in unison, "Sorry, Momma, we'll be good, Momma."

Immediately Susan leaned against her sister, whispered from the corner of her mouth, "Does not!"

All three women shared a nostalgic smile.

Susan gazed across the yard where dozens of scampering children played. Scattered among youngsters from the town and neighboring ranchers were her beloved niece and nephews. Bobby, Laura's oldest son, was five, and a real dynamo of activity who was now teaching his three-year-old brother Joey how to play leapfrog with his cousin Heather.

They'd all grown so much since Susan had last seen them. A mist of sheer happiness fogged her vision. She sniffed, dabbed the corner of her eye, then impulsively clutched her sisters in a group hug. "I've missed you both so much."

"I know." Heaving a sigh, Laura kissed Susan's

cheek, swished a sleep-mussed strand of hair from Catrina's face. "I wish we all lived closer."

Catrina's eyes gleamed with mischief. "What are a few miles when one's sister owns a private Learjet?"

"It's Royce's plane," protested Laura.

Shuddering, Susan raised her palms to signal her distaste for the object in question. "The darned thing scares me to death. I'm just grateful he hasn't had the urge to learn how to fly it himself." She slid a glance at Catrina. "I about had a heart attack when I learned that Rick flew the two of you here in a rented Cessna."

"My husband is an excellent pilot, but if the thought of a rented plane upsets you so much, you can always buy us a Learjet of our own." Catrina grinned, batted her eyes.

"Buy your own Learjet," Laura replied with a snort. "From what I hear, Rick's architectural firm is reputed to be one of the finest in the country and is now branching into European operations. Not bad, not bad at all."

"Rick's doing well," Catrina conceded with a proud smile. "But what about you and Royce? Burton Technologies has been highlighted as a top stock pick by one of the financial gurus of the country."

Laura shrugged, smiled. "The most important thing is that Royce's gamble on refusing to relocate the company paid off, and a town that had been on the verge of economic collapse is prospering. It took courage for Royce to risk everything for the sake of his employees. I'm so proud of him." Laura turned to Susan. "And look at our dear, pragmatic middle sis, married to a sexy rancher who owns half the danged state."

"Half the county," Susan replied, "not half the state. You always did exaggerate."

"Did not."

"Did too."

"Did not."

"Girls, girls, girls." Catrina giggled. "Anyway, since Montana is a convenient point between New York and California, Jarod will have to scrape a landing strip out on the south pasture so your sisters can visit more often."

"Actually, he mentioned doing just that a few days ago. Family means so much to Jarod. He wants you all to feel this is your home as much as ours because, as far as he's concerned, it is." Susan gazed toward the stables, her heart racing. Only a few more minutes and the centerpiece of today's celebration would be revealed. She was excited, apprehensive.

Shading her eyes, she saw Rick Blaine and Royce Burton exit the stables.

This was it. Susan was so excited she could barely breathe. On cue, Claude jumped onto the porch rail, tail twitching in anticipation. At the same moment, Laura spotted her husband and brother-in-law pausing outside the stable. Both men were gazing in rapt fascination at something unseen from the women's vantage point on the porch.

"What's going on?" Laura asked.

Susan was beside herself. "It's a wonderful surprise. Come on!"

By the time Susan guided her sisters to a spot a few feet from where Danny and baby Samantha watched the racing Roundtree youths, Jarod had also exited the stables leading a magnificent chestnut stallion.

Head high, ears pricked forward, the animal snorted

and pranced sideways, its huge eyes scanning the crowd before its gaze settled on the diminutive youngster standing beside his baby sister's stroller.

The boy glanced toward the stable for a moment, then his attention returned to the racing horses. A split second later he did a double take. His gaze was riveted on the animal his father was leading down the path.

Susan held her breath.

Around them the buzzing crowd fell silent. The Roundtree riders reigned their mounts to a standstill. Every eye was on the magnificent mustang and the trembling young boy standing by the paddock fence.

After what seemed a small eternity, Danny's voice broke the strained silence. "Thunder!"

The horse whinnied a greeting, pranced sideways and would have bolted toward the youngster sprinting up the stable road if Jarod had not kept tight hold of the reins.

"Thunder, Thunder!" Laughing and crying at the same time, Danny flung his arms around the animal's neck. "You brought him home, Dad, you brought him back to me." The boy giggled as Thunder nuzzled his ear. "Is he here for good, forever and ever and ever?"

"Yes, son. Thunder is home now." Jarod's taut shoulders relaxed. He glanced at Susan with relief and joy in his eyes, then returned his attention to his son. "Thunder has grown up quite a bit, just as you have. His manners have improved considerably, since he's spent the past year with the best horse trainer in the country."

"Will I be able to ride him, Dad?"

"When you're ready, son. Thunder has always been your horse. He always will be."

As if to put in his own thoughts on the matter,

Thunder emitted a contented snuffle, and pushed his nose against Danny's chest, sniffing the pocket where the boy had once carried equine treats.

Digging into his own pocket, Jarod extracted a sugar cube, pressed it into Danny's hand. The boy's grin as he fed the coveted cube to the animal that he'd once feared melted Susan's heart.

It had come full circle now. Nightmares, terror, regret and guilt, all were over, all were safely tucked into the past.

With tears of joy and relief in her own eyes, Susan scooped Samantha out of her stroller, balanced the cooing baby in the crook of her arm. "Your brother has just met an old friend," she whispered. "Someday you'll understand how much that means to him."

Rick and Royce joined the three women. Laura slipped into her husband's waiting arms, while Catrina flung her arms around Rick's neck and kissed him so passionately that he blushed.

"Wow," Rick murmured when his wife finally released him. "Not that I'm complaining, mind you, but what brought that on?"

Catrina sighed happily. "I just feel so lucky, that's all."

"You are lucky," Laura murmured, laying her head on Royce's shoulder. "So am I and so is Susan." She paused, winked. "Of course we had to kiss a lot of frogs first."

Royce blinked. "Pardon me, but frog-kissing does not sound like a particularly pleasant or sanitary endeavor."

"It's from an old fairy tale." Shifting her daughter, Susan wiped the baby's drooling rosebud mouth. "The cursed prince is in the body of a frog and is set free by his true love's kiss.''

Royce and Rick exchanged a wary glance, much to their wives' amusement.

Susan's attention wandered up the stable path, toward the husband she adored, the son she cherished and the magnificent stallion whose homecoming had warmed so many hearts.

It had come full cycle, Susan realized, the culmination of every hope, every dream, every fantasy come true. Everyone she loved was safe and happy.

For the first time in Susan's life she was part of something larger than herself. The land was in her blood now. It was her life, her legacy, her home.

The final Cinderella sister had found a prince of her own. And they lived happily ever after.

* * * * *